I0658075

Copyright © 2026 by E. E. Frazer

All rights reserved.

No part of this book may be reproduced in any form or by any electronic or mechanical means, including information storage and retrieval systems, without written permission from the author, except for the use of brief quotations in a book review.

This is a work of fiction. Names, characters, businesses, places, events, locales, and incidents are either the products of the author's imagination or used in a fictitious manner. Any resemblance to actual persons, living or dead, or actual events is purely coincidental.

While the locations mentioned in this novel—including Haesindang Park, Seoul, Boston, and Washington D.C.—are real, the specific events and characters depicted therein are fictional.

ISBN: 979-8-9942589-1-0 (Paperback). ISBN: 979-8-9942589-0-3 (E-book).

Cover design by Meridian Literary House

First Edition: January 2026

Published by: Meridian Literary House, Los Angeles, California.

DEDICATION

To my mother, Faye E. Frazer.

From an early age, she recognized the writer in me, encouraging me to think like a novelist but write as myself. She taught me to tell stories that mirror a world more interconnected than separated and that we must always seek to bridge the distance.

She urged me to chase dreams and, whenever possible, to travel— both physically and mentally. As she often said:

"Mental travel requires no passport or money, simply curiosity about people and culture. Watch the news and listen to the radio with that curiosity in mind, and you can travel the entire world."

This is for you Mom. If only you were alive to see where that curiosity has taken me.

Table of Contents

Respect plays nice. Desire doesn't.

Author's Note

We live in an era where it is easy to practice emotional isolationism—to stay within the safe, sterile borders of what we know. But I believe that travel is the ultimate gateway to knowledge and thus a panacea to emotional isolation. It is the act of stepping out of the familiar to realize that the map is not the territory, and that our way is not the only way.

I am an admirer of South Korea, a place that runs on raw momentum. Seoul hums like it's plugged into its own universe: neon stacked on neon, food stalls firing off memory and spice, nights that move fast but somehow still make room for wonder. And then there is Haesindang Park—audacious, unapologetic, and a vivid reminder that joy doesn't have to whisper.

In writing this novel, I wanted to explore the idea that oceans are only as wide as we let them be. Geographically, the Pacific is massive. But culturally and humanly, oceans have a way of becoming surprisingly small when people truly communicate. When we tear down the walls of our own cultural fortresses, we often find that beauty lives in the very places we were taught to misunderstand.

I write as an American who still believes in our unruly promise—people reaching for each other across time zones and traditions because desire refuses to stay local. If this novel makes you blush, trust me, it's on purpose. The heart learns fast when we tear down our walls and let the world in.

E.E. Frazer

Chapter One: The American

The City of Seoul greets us not with fanfare but with a steady, electric shimmer.

It is a sensory invasion. Crosswalks beep in stylish, rhythmic chirps; bus doors sigh open like they are exhaling the fatigue of the commute; signs stack color on top of color—neon blues, burning reds, toxicity greens—until the street feels newly invented, a place where the sun is merely a suggestion and the light is man-made.

Michael spreads his arms wide as we step off the airport limousine bus, embracing the humidity and the noise as if he ordered all of this on a menu and it has finally been delivered. "Gentlemen," he says, his voice cutting through the hum of traffic. "We have arrived at the future."

He says it loudly, which is his way of believing. Beside him, Damion adjusts his glasses, his smile small and approving, the smile of an architect admiring a well-built arch. Lorenzo is already scanning the passing faces of women, wearing the lovely, dangerous grin of a man already composing a story he will tell later over beers.

I stand a little apart. I keep a paper map of Seoul in my hand, creased and folded into a neat square. I know the phone in my pocket is better—faster, smarter, connected to satellites that can pinpoint my heartbeat from space. But a paper map reminds me that I am allowed to unfold things slowly. It reminds me that getting lost is a geometric possibility, not a system error.

"Gray," Michael barks, slapping my shoulder. "Stop analyzing the topography. We're here."

We hike up to the hostel. It sits atop a set of stairs that gleam like rain even when the sky is bone dry. The lobby smells of industrial detergent and cut limes—a sharp, sterile scent that cuts through the humidity. A corkboard by the reception desk lists free walking tours, late-night noodle places, and handwritten rules penned with the soft authority of a favorite teacher: "Please be quiet after 11. The world can wait."

In our room—four bunks, one window, a view of a tangled alleyway that looks like a live broadcast of a cyberpunk novel—Michael throws himself onto the lower mattress. The springs groan. He clasps his hands behind his head and announces a strategic plan that amounts to doing everything at once.

"The DMZ," he says, counting on his fingers. "Night market. K-pop. And especially Bonchon. I didn't fly twelve hours to pretend the American version is the same thing."

"At least pretend we'll sleep," Damion offers, unpacking his toiletries with military precision.

"We'll sleep when we compare Paris Baguette to Paris Baguette," Lorenzo says, checking his reflection in the small, warped mirror. "A scientific inquiry. Is the croissant truer on native soil, or truer in suburban Boston?"

"Both can be true," I say, half serious. "Truth is usually jurisdictional." The boys groan. "Reverend Gray has entered the chat," Michael says. I smile, but I don't retract it. I am the one who likes to test the edges of a question. My father calls it argument practice; my mother calls it worrying out loud. In a year, law school will call it "billable skills." For now, it's just the way my brain organizes the noise.

We leave the bags and step back into the city, which is somehow brighter now that it knows us. The street produces a café just in time—glossy display case, neat paper-wrapped sandwiches, a spotless blue-and-white logo that looks familiar even in another alphabet. Paris Baguette.

We crowd the glass like students. There's a practiced efficiency to the line: take a tray, choose a pastry, marvel at the gleam on the egg tarts that in the States would never dare to look this unapologetically golden. The cashier places our selections into crinkling sleeves with a precision that feels ceremonial.

We take our little haul outside and stand under the shade of the awning like men who still haven't learned to sit. Lorenzo breaks off a corner of a croissant and holds it up to the light, inspecting the lamination as if listening for an accent. "Flakier," he declares, chewing thoughtfully. "Less sweet. Like it knows we have to work for it. It's not begging for approval."

"And the cream roll?" Michael asks with the seriousness of a federal judge. "Cream has integrity," Damion answers, wiping a speck of white from his lip, surprised into a laugh. "How is that a thing? It actually tastes like milk, not chemicals."

We will end up returning two more times this week, unashamedly comparing this Paris Baguette to the ones we've known in the U.S., joyfully arguing about crumb structure and restraint like we are credentialed pastry critics. It feels like a harmless kind of devotion, and I'm grateful for anything that keeps us gentle with the world.

The afternoon turns into evening before we notice. Somewhere a busker is singing a ballad that might be about the sea, or perhaps about a woman who left on a train. We wander into a restaurant whose windows are polished to their own reflection. The menu is crisp and promising, and the server arrives with banchan like an overture—little dishes arranged as if to teach us the circle of flavor.

When the Bonchon fried chicken lands, it does so with a confidence that stills our conversation. The lacquered skin shines as if born to light, glazed in soy and garlic. The first bite is exact—a deafening crack, then tenderness, then heat that blooms and keeps blooming.

"You're not getting this at home," Michael says, reverent for once. "The Colonel would weep." I nod, already anticipating a stern letter from my stomach. The ulcer arrived last year during finals—a physical manifestation of my father's expectations—and never learned to leave. I pace myself. I try the kimchi because it seems dishonest not to. The spice is not friendly at first, but it tells the truth, striking the tongue with fermentation and fire, and I have always liked the truth even when it makes me cough.

We drift back toward the hostel with the kind of fullness that allows the world to be itself without our commentary. We are four American boys in a city that predates our country by a millennium.

On the stairwell, Michael remembers his itinerary. "Gray," he says—using his serious voice. "Tomorrow, we secure tickets for the DMZ. I looked it up. It's intense."

"The Demilitarized Zone," I say, the definition rolling off my tongue automatically. "The buffer zone between North and South. Four kilometers wide, two hundred and fifty kilometers long. The most heavily militarized border in the world." "Exactly," Michael says. "History. Conflict. Tension. Right up your alley."

I nod. It actually is up my alley. I like borders. I like the idea that a line can be drawn in the dirt, and on one side is one reality, and on the other side is another. It appeals to the part of me that believes in contracts and treaties.

"DMZ tomorrow," Michael confirms. "Day after, temple tour. Then… the coastal thing." "What coastal thing?" I ask, already wary of the tone shift. "The museum without walls," Lorenzo says, smiling too directly to be innocent. He pulls out his phone. "You haven't heard of it?" Damion spares me. "Haesindang Park," he says. "The, uh… famous one."

I stop on the landing. "I'm not sure it's on my list." "Art history," Michael counters, trying on a respectable tone that doesn't fit. "Folklore. Cultural literacy." "It's a park full of—" "Dicks," Lorenzo interrupts, abandoning the pretense. He turns his phone screen toward me.

I look. I blink. I look again.

On the small glowing screen is a photograph of a park bench. But the bench is not a bench. It is a massive, polished, wooden phallus. It is carved with startling anatomical commitment—the heavy, swollen head, the thick veins traversing the shaft, the wood varnished to a high, glistening shine that mimics sweat or anticipation.

"Jesus," I whisper.

"It's not just one," Lorenzo says, swiping the screen. "It's a forest of them, Gray. Look at this." The next photo shows a cannon. But the cannon barrel is a penis, rigid and aggressive, pointed out toward the sea. Swipe. A totem pole of erections, stacked one on top of the other, carved from cedar that looks warm and fleshy in the sunlight. Swipe. A statue of a fisherman, joyfully clutching a member that is larger than his own torso, the glans carved with a level of detail that feels aggressive.

"It's a fertility shrine," Michael says, trying to sound academic but failing as a giggle escapes him. "It's a penis park," Lorenzo corrects. "It's acres of wood, stone, and plastic, all hard, all huge, all pointed at the ocean. Look at this one. It's literally a lighthouse. A dick lighthouse."

I look at the image. It is, indeed, a lighthouse shaped like a phallus, red and throbbing against the blue sky. I feel a heat rising up the back of my neck. It's not just prudishness; it's a physical reaction to the sheer, overwhelming explicitness of it. It's the brazen lack of privacy. In my world—in Boston, in the firm, in my father's house—sex is something that happens in the dark, behind locked doors, and is never, ever carved into wood and displayed for tourists.

"Why?" I ask. "Why would anyone do this?" "Legend says a virgin died there," Damion says quietly. "She drowned. The fish stopped coming. The fishermen pissed in the water, and the fish came back. So… they figured the male essence appeased her spirit."

"So they built a park of giant cocks to comfort a dead virgin?" I ask, my voice rising. "That is… that is grotesque."

"It's hilarious," Lorenzo says. "And we are going. Come on, Gray. Imagine the photos. Imagine standing next to a six-foot piece of timber carved into a perfect erection. You can sit on them. You can touch them. They sell bread shaped like them, filled with white cream."

My stomach turns, the earlier pastry suddenly feeling heavy. The imagery is too vivid. I can picture the texture of the wood—smooth, worn down by thousands of hands. I can imagine the smell of the sea mixed with the absurdity of this sexual landscape. It feels lawless. It feels like a violation of public order.

"I'm not going," I say stiffly. "You have to," Michael says. "It's culture." "It's pornography," I counter. "It's landscape pornography." "It's a park full of symbols near the sea," Michael insists, delighted.

I understand humor; I even sometimes allow it. But I have spent most of my life being careful with the boundary between reverence and ridicule. This sounds like a field trip designed to trample the line, unzip it, and wave it around in the fresh air. I say, "I'll think about it," which in my family is how you keep the peace when your answer is absolutely no.

Downstairs, the lobby has softened into its evening voice. I need to get away from the boys. I need to get away from the mental images of polished cedar veins and cream-filled pastries.

A girl sits at the corner table with a sketchbook. The contrast is immediate and striking. If the conversation upstairs was a chaotic, crude scrawl, she is fine calligraphy. Her hair gathers the lamplight and gives it back as if she rehearsed it. She is drawing quickly, the kind of quick that comes from patience, her hand moving with a fluidity that suggests she knows exactly where the line needs to end.

For a moment, I allow myself the luxury of watching someone be good at what they love. It calms the static in my head. It washes away the image of the lighthouse. She looks up and catches me. I freeze, prepared for the cool dismissal I usually get from women this beautiful. But she isn't accusing. Her look is more like, Yes, you are here, too. We are both awake. I almost say sorry. She smiles, the moth-wing kind—soft, fluttering, barely there—that says it isn't necessary.

We meet again in the morning as if we rehearsed it. The lobby is empty. The morning light is gray and soft. She is at the kettle squeezing lemon into a cup, her movements precise. Her eyes are careful and warm. "Tea?" she asks. "Yes," I say, because I am still the sort of man who says yes formally to kindness. "American?" she ventures. Her accent is faint, musical. "I'm trying to hide it," I answer, which is my version of a joke. She laughs softly. "You're doing very well. You stand very still. Americans usually fidget." "I'm Edward." I should say I'm pleased to meet you, but I can tell she would rather do the actual meeting than narrate it. "Jennie," she says. The name settles into the room as if it's owned the table all along.

There is a brief negotiation with silence, the kind that permits two strangers to exist in the same square feet without pretending to be anything else. I watch her hands around the mug. They are stained with charcoal.

Then Michael sweeps in, trailing the weather and his loud energy. "Field trip," he declares, clapping his hands. He nods to Jennie as though she has co-signed our itinerary. "We're going to the DMZ," Damion tells her, respectful. "Any advice? You're local, right?" "Listen more than you talk," she says, looking at her tea. "History keeps a low voice sometimes. It's a sad place, not just a photo op." I nod. I like that answer.

"And the coast?" Lorenzo asks, bouncing on the balls of his feet, smiling too cheerfully. He pulls out his phone again. I tense up. I pray he doesn't show her the photos. I pray he doesn't flash the carved wooden members in her face. "We're thinking of Haesindang," Lorenzo says, winking at me.

I look at the floor. I am mortified. I am prepared to apologize on behalf of my entire gender. Jennie's eyes flick toward me, then to Lorenzo, and back to me. She sees my discomfort. She sees the red flush creeping up my neck.

"The coast is good," she says evenly. Her voice doesn't change. She doesn't giggle. She doesn't look scandalized. "There is a park there that people visit to laugh and to remember. If you go, do both."

I look up. She isn't mocking it. Michael's delighted clap is a small storm. "See? Educational! Jennie approves. Reverend Gray, you'll give the benediction." I try to rescue my dignity. "I doubt I'm the right officiant for… that kind of congregation."

Jennie studies me. Her gaze is direct, stripping away my defense. "You don't have to like something to learn from it," she says. "The park is… explicit, yes. It is honest about what it is. It doesn't hide. You should stand in front of it before you decide."

Stand in front of it. She isn't talking about the wood. She is talking about the honesty. The raw, unvarnished, erect truth of the place. I tell myself I am going for the coastline, for the legend I half-remember reading about—something to do with a drowned maiden and fishermen carving a future out of grief. I tell myself I am going because travel is the disciplined practice of curiosity.

But when I try to picture the park now, I don't just see the crude photos on Lorenzo's phone. I see the way Jennie spoke about it. I see the possibility that something can be salacious and sacred at the same time. I pray, as is my habit, not for permission but for clarity: Help me see what is in front of me and not what I brought with me.

Then I fold the paper map until it remembers how to become a small square of intention, and I follow my friends into a morning that smells like coffee and lemons and dangerous possibilities.

Chapter Two: Jennie

Some faces arrive noisy before the mouth even opens. They announce themselves with the friction of their movement, demanding the room rearrange itself to accommodate their energy.

His did not.

He entered the hostel lobby like a footnote the paragraph was lucky to have—present, precise, uninterested in stealing the sentence. The loud one (Michael, I would learn) invented applause at random intervals, treating Seoul like a stage he had rented for the week. The easy one (Lorenzo) flirted with the architecture, with gravity, with the idea of lunch. The quiet one (Damion) watched like a good editor, editing the chaos of his friends.

And Edward—Edward measured the room as though he planned to pay for any attention he spent.

I sat in the corner, charcoal dust on my fingertips, sketching the way the light hit the scuffed linoleum floor. I like to draw before I speak. It organizes the weather inside my head. The common room was a good subject: a plant that refused to give up despite the lack of sun, a wall of postcards curling at the edges, and an electric kettle that hissed like a piano teaching scales to steam.

I sketched them quickly while the light behaved. Then I sketched him. Just the line of his shoulders—tight, held high, carrying an invisible weight.

When he came over for hot water, I offered him a slice of lemon. Not because he asked, but because lemon suits careful people; it asks nothing and gives brightness. "Tea?" I asked. "Yes," he said. He didn't just say the word; he formally submitted it. "American?" "I'm trying to hide it." I laughed. "You're doing very well. You stand very still. Americans usually fidget."

He told me his name was Edward. He said it the way you place a heavy book on a table—carefully, ensuring it doesn't make a sound. He called me Jennie like he had tasted the name first to be sure it wasn't poisonous.

Then his friends descended, a storm of maps and itinerary debates. They asked about the DMZ. Tourists always ask about the DMZ. They want the thrill of the border, the proximity to danger. I gave them the gentle instructions tourists deserve: bring patience, lower your voice, allow history its unspectacular truth.

Then the one called Lorenzo brought up the coast. "Haesindang," he said, grinning.

I froze for a micro-second, my charcoal hovering over the page. To them, it was a joke. A punchline. A park full of penises near the ocean. To me, it was the familiar mixture—humor drawing a circle around grief so it won't run the town.

"The coast is good," I said, looking at Edward. I saw the flush rise on his neck. He was mortified. He looked like a man who wanted to apologize to the air for the existence of anatomy. "There is a park there that people visit to laugh and to remember. If you go, do both."

Edward looked terrified. He tried to back out of it with a joke about being the wrong officiant. I studied him. I saw the fear. He was afraid of being undignified. He was afraid of the messiness of being human. "You don't have to like something to learn from it," I told him. "But you should stand in front of it before you decide."

It was a dare. He nodded the way good students nod when they are deciding whether to keep being good or try being brave.

I grew up not far from that coast. The East Sea is different from the calm waters of the West. It is deeper, colder, bluer. It doesn't forgive mistakes.

When I was twelve, the sea took my brother, Jun-ho. It wasn't a storm. It wasn't a tragedy that made the national news. It was just a cramp, or a current, or a miscalculation. One minute he was bobbing in the waves, laughing, shouting for me to look at him. The next, the water was smooth and empty.

We learned the practicalities of absence that summer. My father learned to pull the cork from a bottle of soju when the wind sounded too much like a boy's voice. My mother learned to call cooking a "storm drill," making enough food for neighbors who were not hungry, just so the house would smell like life instead of death.

And I learned about Haesindang. The legend of the park is about a virgin who drowned, Aue-bawi. The fishermen couldn't catch fish because her spirit was angry, grieving the life she never lived. They tried rituals. They tried prayers. Nothing worked. Until a fisherman, desperate and angry, relieved himself into the ocean. The fish returned. The village decided that her spirit wasn't angry; it was lonely. It wanted the male essence. So, they carved the wood. They made the phalluses. They made them big, funny, grotesque, and beautiful. They filled the cliffside with them to comfort a dead girl.

It sounds obscene to outsiders. But where I come from, it makes sense. Grief is a void. You have to fill it with something—something loud, something life-affirming, something that screams we are still here, we are still bodies, we are still alive. Children laugh at the park because laughter is how you carry weight without breaking. Elders nod because rituals—even odd ones—give shape to what the tide refuses to explain.

I wanted Edward to see that. I wanted to see if the boy with the stiff shoulders could look at the absurdity of grief and not turn away.

The next morning, I packed my bag out of habit, not need. The sky was clean, the way new notebooks are clean. The city had its own grammar: crosswalk, pause; subway, shoulder; café, tray.

I stopped at Paris Baguette on the way to the hostel. I bought a sweet roll—soft bread filled with fresh cream. I stood in the line and thought about the American version Edward talked about. He spoke of "crumb structure" and "lamination" like they were religious doctrines. He treated pleasure like it was something that had to be audited.

In my art class, Professor Park always asks us where sincerity and performance intersect. "Here," I say, pointing to my chest. Edward was all performance. He was wearing a suit even when he was wearing jeans. But I had seen a glimpse of sincerity when he drank the tea. I wanted to see more.

By afternoon, I was back at the hostel covering the desk for Soo-mi. The boys came in like weather warnings—good ones. They had purchased paper maps, treating them like ancient artifacts. They stood around the table like a planning committee, arguing in cheerful murmurs about train transfers and window seats.

Edward stood a little apart. He kept touching the folded square of the map in his pocket as if it were a promise he wanted to make properly. He lingered when the others went to fetch their jackets. "Why is it important?" he asked me. His eyes were not yet practiced at hiding his confusion. "The park. Why did you insist?"

Because it names what we are made of, I thought. Because it turns panic into art. Because sometimes you have to laugh at the cathedral of the body before you can kneel in it honestly.

Aloud, I said, "Because it's honest about us. About wanting. About bodies. About how we pretend we're above the very thing that built us. The park doesn't pretend." He absorbed that with a stillness I respected. "I was taught to be careful." "So was I," I said, and smiled. "I was also taught to feed people. Food is a kind of truth."

I reached into my bag and handed him the sweet roll I bought. The plastic crinkled in the quiet lobby. "For your research," I said. He looked at the bread, then at me. He laughed—not loudly, but like a person who recognizes a blessing that isn't dressed as one. "You didn't have to." "I know," I said. "That's why it counts."

We studied each other for a breath. Not romantically, not yet. Like travelers sharing a compass no one will admit they lost. Then Michael swept back in, trailing noise and urgency, and the moment folded itself up like the map in Edward's pocket.

That night, I lay in my narrow bed and listened to the street find its hush. My phone buzzed. It was Sohee.

Sohee: Are you going to the coast with the Americans? Jennie: Just for the day. To show them the route. Sohee: Be careful. Tourists break things. They treat people like souvenirs. Jennie: He's different. Sohee: They're never different, Jennie. They just have different accents.

She sent a sardonic cartoon of a girl waiting for a train that never comes. She texted: Don't fall for anyone who says sorry before they speak. I sent back a line drawing I did on my tablet—a man holding an apology like an umbrella. She awarded it three knives and a heart.

Sleep was slow to arrive. I inventoried my small hopes: that the weather would hold; that the light would arrive sideways on the cliffs the way it sometimes does; that the boys would understand it is possible to be irreverent and reverent in the same hour without collapsing into hypocrisy.

I thought of Jun-ho. I thought of how he would have tormented me with jokes about the park until I threw a sandal at his head. I thought of my father, staring at his glass, and how he would never come with us but would ask me afterward if the sea looked like it was listening.

Morning was a neat envelope. I met them on the platform. Their faces were bright with the particular optimism of men who have not yet been defeated by ticket machines in a language they respect but cannot decipher. Edward saw me and looked surprised that I kept my promise. Then relieved. Then something else I decided to name focus.

On the train, the city gave way to its quieter cousins—warehouses, then rice fields, then startled mountains rising up to meet the tracks. The boys discussed the Paris Baguette findings with a rigor that would impress a thesis advisor. Flavor ratios were debated. Michael declared the Bonchon we ate "a spiritual experience" and looked at me, half daring me to call it blasphemy. "It's allowed," I said. "Some churches serve better chicken than sermons."

Edward's laugh was quick and unguarded. He leaned his head against the window, watching the blur of green and gray. He looked like he was trying to solve the equation of the landscape. I wanted to tell him: The deciding is not the point, Edward. The showing up is.

We reached the coast by midday. The air changed instantly. It became the kind of air that keeps secrets until it trusts you—salty, cold, abrasive. The sea looked busy, whitecaps chopping the surface as if the water was late for a meeting.

We followed the path toward the park. It announced itself the way parades do—not with subtlety, but with an excellent memory for human delight. Even before the statues came into view, the laughter did. I heard a group of ajummas ahead of us, cackling wildly as they posed next to a wooden bench carved like a giant phallus. It wasn't cruel laughter. It wasn't the snickering of adolescents. It was the belly-laugh of women who have birthed children, buried husbands, and survived wars. It was the laughter of survival.

I watched Edward take it in. We rounded the corner, and there it was. A forest of erections. Totem poles. Benches. Cannons. A lighthouse. All carved with loving, explicit detail. Michael and Lorenzo lost their minds immediately. They ran toward the statues, phones out, posing, joking, entranced by the sheer audacity of it.

Edward stood still. He looked at the first sculpture—a massive piece of driftwood smoothed into a distinct shape. He looked at the second—a whimsical face carved into the glans of another. He didn't laugh. But he didn't run away. He looked at the plaque that told the story of Aue-bawi. He read every word.

I walked up beside him. The wind whipped my hair across my face. "Art," I said softly, "is just an argument you make with sincerity." He turned to me. His face was open, unguarded for the first time. "And this is… sincere?" he asked. Not mocking me. Not mocking it. Just asking.

"It began with grief," I said, looking out at the water where my brother's ghost still sometimes swam. "The rest is just how people lived with the story. They took the most life-affirming thing they knew—sex, creation, pleasure—and used it to fight death."

He nodded. His eyes found whatever they needed to find in the wood and the water. He is not a man who will touch a thing until he has decided he can do so without lying. There is a formality to him that I used to think was a uniform, until I learned it is, in fact, a kindness he offers the world: to take it seriously.

"Thank you," he said. "For what?" "For making me look."

"You're welcome," I answered. And because I am built this way—to push, just a little—I added, "Now let's see if you can laugh and not apologize to the air for laughing."

He looked at Lorenzo, who was straddling a wooden cannon and shouting orders to an imaginary navy. Edward smiled. Then he chuckled. Then he laughed—a real sound, carried away by the wind. He did not apologize. The sea kept moving. And the park, which has watched all of us for years—the grieving, the curious, the lonely—

18

looked briefly pleased. Like a teacher whose students have finally stopped whispering and started listening.

Chapter Three: Haesindang Park

Fantasy Meets Temptation -There is a moment, standing at the edge of the path where the gravel turns to dirt, when the park stops being a rumor on Lorenzo's phone and arranges itself into a physical thesis. The ocean is on our left, a vast, indifferent slate of blue crashing against the cliffs. The wind is aggressive, salt-heavy, editing our hair without permission.

And ahead of us is the wood.

It is not subtle. It does not ease you in. The first sculptures rise from the sloping grass like a hallucination. They are massive. They are polished by weather and countless hands until they shine like bone. They are, undeniably, aggressively, phalluses.

My first reaction is physical. A heat rises up the back of my neck, a primal, Puritanical flush that feels like a sunburn. My stomach gives a hard twist, the ulcer waking up to register a formal protest. It is one thing to see a crude JPEG on a phone screen in a hostel lobby; it is another to stand in front of a ten-foot tall totem pole carved in the distinct, unmistakable shape of an erection, complete with veins that twine around the cedar like ivy.

"Holy shit," Lorenzo whispers, the words reverent and profane all at once.

It is an assault on propriety. In the world I come from—the world of mahogany boardrooms and hushed country clubs and suits buttoned tight against the throat—sex is a shadow. It is something that happens behind locked doors, something alluded to but never named.

Here, it is named, shouted, and carved into the landscape. There are benches shaped like penises. There are railings held up by them. There are wind chimes that clank together, dangling wooden members. There are statues of fishermen clutching phalluses larger than their own torsos, grinning maniacally at the sea.

"This is… aggressive," I manage to say, my voice tighter than I intend. "It's magnificent," Michael counters, already pulling out his phone. He runs toward a statue that doubles as a cannon barrel.

"Gray, get a picture of me straddling this. The guys back home are going to lose their minds."

I look away. I feel a profound, disorienting embarrassment—not just for myself, but for the wood, for the ocean, for the sheer lack of shame on display. It feels lawless. It feels like a place where the rules of civilization have been suspended.

I look for Jennie. She is walking a few steps ahead, her camera slung diagonally across her chest like a practical sentence. She isn't giggling. She isn't pointing. She isn't averting her eyes. She is moving like someone who has made peace with this place and is waiting for us to catch up.

She stops at a large bronze plaque set into a stone near the entrance. I walk toward her, grateful for a moment of text, something I can analyze. I fall into a rhythm at her side—close enough to speak without shouting over the wind, far enough to mean it as a courtesy.

"I'm trying to understand," I tell her, keeping my eyes on the horizon and away from the towering wooden member to my right, "where reverence ends and performance begins." "Maybe they hold hands," she says, looking at the plaque. "Maybe the point is that you can't have one without the other."

A local guide, compact and steady, wearing a windbreaker that has seen better decades, notices our hesitation near the plaque. He approaches, his face a roadmap of wrinkles. "Long time ago," he says in English, his voice gravelly, glancing at the water as if the past might surface. "A young woman—Aue-bawi—she fall from a boat. Drowned. Virgin."

He says the word virgin with a clinical detachment. "After she die, the fishermen, they catch no fish. The village is hungry. They think her spirit is angry because she never…" He makes a vague gesture with his hands, a universal sign for union. "She never know a man."

I feel my jaw tighten. It feels grotesque. A village blaming their starvation on the sexual frustration of a dead girl. "So they made offerings," the guide continues. "To soothe the sea. To soothe her. They carve the wood. The big wood. They put it here, looking at the ocean. And the fish come back."

21

He doesn't wink. He doesn't lower his voice. He speaks as if telling us the history of a suspension bridge. He gestures to the hillside covered in hundreds—maybe thousands—of carvings. "These are… how do you say… reminders. Protection. Hope. You laugh, yes. But you also eat fish." He nods once, satisfied with his explanation, and walks away.

I am left staring at the plaque. It is a story of grief, starvation, and a desperate, almost magical attempt to bargain with death using the only life-affirming symbol they had. Intellectually, I understand it. Emotionally, I am still standing in a park full of giant wooden dicks.

"Best history lesson ever," Michael whispers to Damion. Damion nudges him, a gentle governor on the engine.

We move deeper into the park. The path winds up the cliffside. Every turn reveals a new variation on the theme. Some are whimsical—faces carved into the glans, smiling beatifically. Some are functional—a zodiac clock where every animal is riding a phallus. Some are just… massive. Undeniable blocks of wood dedicated to a single purpose.

Lorenzo calls for a picture. "Group shot," he announces, having found a cluster of statues arranged like a choir. "Proof of cultural literacy." "I'll take it," Jennie offers.

The three of us—four with Damion—stand together in a line in front of the wooden choir. I don't know where to put my hands. I don't know where to look. I feel ridiculous. I feel exposed. I feel like a man in a suit at a nudist colony. Michael throws one arm around me and the other around Lorenzo and squeezes hard. For a second, the sheer physical camaraderie breaks through my defenses. We are simply boys again, learning how to smile at the world without asking it to rearrange itself for our benefit.

Jennie checks the screen. "Good. Now you." She turns the lens toward me. "One more," she says. "Just you. And a piece of the story."

I start to refuse. Refusal has always been my polite reflex. No thank you, I'm fine. No thank you, I don't need anything. But she is already stepping back to find the angle, her face serious behind the camera. She gestures toward a large, dark figure carved from weathered oak. It stands taller than me, brooding over the cliff edge. It is less cartoonish than the others, more elemental.

The thing about being seen by someone sincere is that it feels less like exposure and more like agreement. I walk over to the figure. I do not touch it. I stand next to it, feeling the heat of the sun on the dark wood. I don't look at the camera. I look at the horizon beyond it, where the sea meets the sky in a hazy line. The wind does what it wants with my hair.

I think of my mother, in her quiet kitchen in Boston, lighting candles for people whose names I never learned, murmuring prayers into the silence. I think of my father, setting down a glass of scotch with the finality of a gavel after winning an argument at the dinner table that no one else knew was happening. I think of the rigidity of my life, the careful lines I have drawn around myself.

And here I am. Standing next to a giant wooden erection on a Korean cliffside, while a girl with charcoal on her fingers takes my picture.

The shutter clicks. My throat does something complicated. A tightness that isn't fear, but something closer to release. "What will you do with it?" I ask, my voice rougher than I expect. Jennie lowers the camera. Her eyes are clear, unsmiling, kind. "Remember," she says.

We walk on. Michael and Lorenzo have moved to the "Cannon Penises," a section that invites—no, demands—slapstick humor. I hear them shouting, pretending to fire on passing fishing boats. Damion lingers over a plaque explaining the different types of cedar used.

I walk with Jennie to the overlook at the very top of the park. Here, the carvings are fewer. The focus is the view. The cliffs drop sharply to the churning water below. It suggests a polite, terrifying ending to the land. We do not talk for a minute. The ocean is doing too much talking to be interrupted.

"You believe in God," she says at last. It is not a question, but I treat it like one. It is the kind of statement she makes that feels like she has read my file. "I do." "And you think God minds this?" She gestures vaguely at the park behind us, at the laughter drifting up the hill.

I consider this. I think about the God of my father—a God of rules, of judgment, of buttoned-up shirts and quiet Sundays. A God who would burn this park to the ground. Then I think about the God I sometimes feel when I am alone—a God of vastness, of ocean, of strange biology and messy humanity.

"I think God minds cruelty," I say slowly, testing the words. "I think God minds contempt. This… this doesn't feel like either. It feels… human. It feels desperate and embarrassing and brave, all at once." She nods, looking out at the water. The quiet that follows is not the awkward sort. It is the honest kind, the kind that comes after a true thing has been said.

We leave the park when the light has made a promise to the late afternoon, turning the sky into bruised purple and orange. On the path back toward town, a vendor sells paper cups of roasted chestnuts. The smell is warm and earthy, cutting through the salt air. Jennie buys a bag. She tips the hot, peel-your-own nuts into my cupped hands. Our palms touch for a second. Her skin is cool.

"To Aue-bawi," Michael yells, holding up a chestnut like a shot glass. "May she finally be getting some peace." Lorenzo laughs. Even I smile. It feels like a harmless prayer.

We find a small restaurant that leans against the street like an old friend, windows steamed from the inside. It is crowded, noisy, and smells incredible—garlic, chili, and the ocean. Inside, tables are polished by time and elbows. A fan on the wall turns too slowly to matter but fast enough to prove it cares. The menu is the kind you don't overthink: fresh if the sea says so, spicy because that's how the body remembers it is alive.

I let someone else order. For a man whose life is a series of carefully weighed decisions, it feels good, for once, to surrender a choice and call it wisdom.

As we wait for the food, Jennie takes out her camera. She scrolls through the day's work, the screen glowing between us. She tilts it toward me without ceremony. There we are: the group shot, the four of us grinning like idiots against a backdrop of phalluses, looking like we don't know how to be unhappy. Then, the next photo.

It's me. Standing by the dark oak figure. I am not looking at the camera. My hands are in my pockets. The wind is blowing my hair back from my face. I don't recognize the expression. It is not defensive. It is not arrogant. It is not surrendering. It is the look of a man who has stopped fighting the current for just a second. It is the look of someone listening.

"You made me look kinder than I am," I say quietly. "No," she answers, looking at the photo, not me. "I made you look the way you were for a second. That counts more."

When the food arrives, it does so all at once, a deluge of small plates and steaming pots, as if the kitchen rejects the notion of courses. The table disappears under bowls of red stew, glossy grilled eel, mountain vegetables, and five different kinds of kimchi. The eel—jang-eo—shines with a soy glaze that looks lacquered on. The kimchi looks like someone dared fire to become cabbage and it accepted the challenge. The first sip of makgeolli—the milky rice wine served in metal bowls—is soft and surprising, fizzing slightly on the tongue like bread trying on a new job.

I am careful, yes. My ulcer is a constant, low-level hum in my gut. But I am not so careful that caution steals the scene. I try everything. I let the spice burn. I let the textures surprise me. "You okay?" Jennie asks. Not hovering. Not mothering. Just checking the instrumentation. "I am," I tell her, and I mean it. The food feels honest. It feels like fuel. "I'd like to learn how you taste the world."

She smiles, picking up a piece of eel with her chopsticks. "You start with what people make when they're tired," she says. "Or what they make when they're grieving. That's where the truth lives."

Michael pronounces the eel superior to every protein he has ever ingested. Lorenzo, already thinking about the next meal, maps out a café known for elaborate shaved ice. Damion leans back against the wall, letting contentment do its slow, useful work. I sit amid the noise and the steam and the strange language, feeling an inexplicable sense of home. Then I realize: perhaps home is not a place on a map.

Perhaps home is just any place where you can pay attention without fear.

When the bill comes, I reach for it automatically. It is my reflex—to pay, to provide, to control the transaction. Jennie shakes her head. Her hand covers mine on the check. "No," she says simply. "You can get the coffee. Let me buy you this lesson."

In my family, generosity is often confused with leverage. A gift is an obligation waiting to be called in. Here, in this noisy restaurant by the sea, it feels like an ordinary exchange of care. I accept. It feels like setting down a heavy book I didn't realize I was carrying.

After dinner, we step out into the night air. It smells faintly of salt, roasted chestnuts, and something sweet I can't name. The street hums with life—couples walking arm in arm, teenagers laughing near a claw machine arcade, fishermen smoking cigarettes by the harbor. It is a life that is not waiting for us, but seems willing to welcome us anyway.

Jennie presses a folded receipt into my hand. On the back, she has written the name of a café and drawn an arrow like a blessing. "We should go," she says. "Lorenzo is right about the dessert. It's a small cathedral of ice." I laugh. It's a real laugh, startled out of me. "And the sermon?" "Short," she says, delighted. "It just says: eat something sweet before the dark gets too big. You'll love it."

I do. Not only the dessert—a mountain of impossibly fine shaved ice that dissolves on the tongue like a kind decision, topped with fruit that shines with its own permission—but the fact of sitting across from her in a quiet corner, talking in sentences that don't require decoration or defense.

She asks about law school the way people ask about the weather: aware that it shapes your day even if you cannot control it. I tell her I plan to go in the fall. That I like the clean lines of argument, the architecture of logic. That I struggle with how easily those lines can be drawn to enclose the wrong things. "And your family?" she asks, gentler there. "Exacting," I say, choosing the word carefully. "Loving in a way that often sounds like instruction." She nods slowly, looking at her spoon, as if that answer arrived exactly on time.

When we walk back toward the train station, the sky has decided to try on indigo. Michael and Lorenzo argue amicably ahead of us about whether humor travels better across cultures than love does. Damion solves nothing and looks pleased to be listening. I stay close to Jennie. I do not pretend this day was ordinary. I do not pretend I am the same person who stepped off the train this morning. I do not know what it is. I only know that something in me has moved—the way a rusty hinge moves when it finally learns it can open without coming off the door.

On the train back to Seoul, the car is quiet. People sleep sitting up, heads lolling with the motion of the train. The city outside the window glows like a memory already rehearsing itself. I close my eyes. In prayer, I used to ask for certainty. I used to ask for the right path to be illuminated. Tonight, I ask for room. Room to look at the messy, embarrassing, sacred world. Room to laugh without apology. Room to love something I do not completely understand and call that reverence instead of failure.

Chapter Four: The Grammar of Loss

Jennie

The park lingers in the body the way a joke lingers after you've stopped laughing: the noise is gone, but the warmth remains in your chest.

We step into the restaurant, a place that smells of grilled charcoal and fermented chili, and the shift is immediate. The wind is behind us. The sea is behind us. Now, there is only the immediate, demanding hunger of four American boys who have spent the afternoon contemplating mortality and anatomy.

Michael and Lorenzo fall in love instantly with the table. They are enchanted by the sheer physics of it—how the server manages to slide more metal bowls onto the surface than geometry should allow. They treat the banchan like a puzzle, poking at the acorn jelly and the fish cakes with delighted suspicion.

I pretend not to notice how they pretend not to stare when I order. I choose the jang-eo—freshwater eel—and a kimchi stew pungent enough to clear a room. It is a test. Not a cruel one, but a necessary one. I need to know who they are when they are out of their depth.

Edward watches everything. He sits across from me, his coat folded neatly next to him. He doesn't look like a scholar or a brother or a guest. He looks like a man trying to memorize a language he doesn't speak yet.

When the food arrives, steam rising in aggressive clouds, Edward tastes carefully. He doesn't rush. He puts the eel in his mouth as if respect has a flavor. When the heat from the kimchi hits—a sharp, red spike of capsaicin—color floods his cheeks. His eyes water. But he doesn't run for his water glass. He waits. He finds his breath. He lets the burn settle.

I feel an unexpected tenderness toward his effort. It would be easy for him to make a joke of it, to perform the "helpless foreigner" routine that Michael is currently enacting with a piece of spicy radish. But Edward isn't proving anything. He isn't demanding a medal. He is simply making space inside himself for something new.

"Good?" I ask, because checking in is a form of translation. "More than good," he says, his voice raspy. The answer lands softly.

It would be easy to keep this dynamic: me as the local guide, him as the humble tourist. That is a safe table to set. But I look at his face— still flushed, still open from the park—and I decide to clear the table. I decide to talk to him the way I talk to people I intend to keep.

"My brother loved this," I say, gesturing to the glossy, grilled eel. "He said it tasted like bravery pretending to be food."

The table noise—Michael arguing with Lorenzo about baseball, Damion laughing—fades into the background. Edward puts his chopsticks down. He doesn't ask the polite, American follow-up questions (Oh, where is he? what does he do?). He nods in a way that says: I hear the part you didn't say.

"Was he older or younger?" Edward asks softly.

"Younger," I say. "By three years. He was the loud one. I was the quiet one."

"And was he—" Edward stops. He catches himself. He looks at me, and I see the precise moment his mind edits the sentence. "Is he funny?"

My chest tightens. It is a small thing. A tiny grammatical shift. But it changes the world. He moved the verb from the past tense to the present tense. He understood, without me having to explain, that in my family, Jun-ho is not a was. He is an is. He is a silence at the table, a shadow in the hallway, a laugh we still hear when the wind hits the windows.

"Very," I say, my voice thick. "He would have made twelve jokes today before noon. He would have climbed the statues. He would have gotten us kicked out by one o'clock."

"Then I'm glad we honored him with at least eight jokes," Edward says, glancing at Michael, who is currently trying to toast the table with a piece of lettuce. "And that we didn't get kicked out."

I look at Edward. Really look at him. Sohee warned me about tourists. She said they consume and leave. But this man isn't consuming. He is witnessing.

We walk after the meal because walking is how the body helps the heart file what it just learned. On the promenade, the wind is working late, whipping the sea into whitecaps. The boys drift ahead, drawn like moths to a street vendor selling fish cakes on skewers.

Edward and I slow down near a signboard detailing the origin story of the park—the legend of Aue-bawi. The English translation is earnest, slightly sideways, full of words like "appease" and "virile." Edward reads every word. He doesn't skim. When he finishes, he takes out his phone. I watch him type the names—Aue-bawi, Haesindang—into a note on his phone. He types them carefully, checking the spelling against the sign.

"You're a good student," I say, tightening my scarf. "I don't want to be a lazy tourist," he answers, pocketing the phone. "I've been that before. It didn't fit. It felt like wearing shoes on the wrong feet." "What does fit?"

He considers the question. He looks out at the dark water, where the lights of squid boats are bobbing on the horizon. "Listening," he says finally. "And laughing when laughter is the right size."

The light from the streetlamp catches the angle of his jaw. He looks tired, but clear. I raise my camera. Usually, I ask. Usually, I stage. But the light is doing something generous to his face, softening the rigid lines of his worry. He startles slightly at the lens, then allows it. He doesn't pose. He just stands there. I frame him with the sea behind him, the park just off to the right in the shadows. I capture that particular expression he wears—the look of a man who thinks he should apologize for existing, and then remembers, just for a second, that he doesn't need to.

Click. I take the photograph because the moment is not mine if I don't. He steps beside me to see the screen. The image glows in the twilight. "I look…" He trails off. "Unarmed?" I offer. He looks at me, surprised by the accuracy. "Unarmed," he repeats. "That's rare. I'm usually wearing armor." "Keep it," I say. I tap the screen and send it to his phone.

He glances down at the notification. Something private happens behind his eyes—a softening, a crack in the foundation. I do not pry. I let him have the room.

The café I chose after dinner is small on purpose. It is a refuge from the wind. We order bingsu—shaved milk ice topped with sweet red beans and condensed milk. It arrives like a small, edible mountain. We share it the way strangers share a bench during a storm: carefully, grateful for the cover.

The sugar hits us, waking us up. He tells me about his law school plans. He speaks of it not with excitement, but with duty. He talks about "clean arguments" and "precedent." He says he worries that truth doesn't always come packaged in clean lines. "The cleanest art is often the least honest," I tell him. "If you can see all the lines, the artist is probably lying to you." He nods, absorbing this as if I put a book on a shelf he'd been building in his mind.

"You're patient with me," he says after a while, scooping up a spoonful of melting ice. "I am with anyone who tries," I answer. "It's the people who decide not to try that wear me out." He meets my eyes. He does not promise anything. He does not swear he will always try. He just holds my gaze. It feels like the correct size of vow.

On the train back to Seoul, the car is warm and rhythmic. Michael and Lorenzo are debating which Paris Baguette pastry will mean the most to them in twenty years, arguing as if nostalgia can be selected by committee. Damion has fallen asleep, his head resting against the window, looking younger than he is.

Edward sits across from me. The train sways as it rounds a curve in the mountains. Our knees touch. It is a small contact. Denim against denim. He doesn't move his knee. I don't move mine. We hold that pose for ten miles. Twenty. The darkness rushes past the window, but the heat at that small point of contact anchors us. It is a conversation without words. It says: I am here. I am not pulling away.

We arrive back at the hostel late. The lobby is quiet, the "Please be quiet" sign presiding over the empty room. Before we part at the

31

stairs, he stops. "Jennie," he says. "Yes?" "May I send the photograph to my mother?"

I understand what he means instantly. He isn't sending a travel update. He wants to tell her: I was safe. I was good. I stood in front of the strange thing and did not flinch. He wants to tell her: I met someone who made me think without making me into a project.

"Of course," I tell him. "Tell her the sea was listening." He smiles. A real one. "Was it?" "It always is," I say.

I head upstairs before my voice tells on me. Before I say something reckless, like Stay.

In bed, the city murmurs outside like an old friend trying not to wake the house. I open my camera roll. I look at him again. Unarmed. There is a version of this story where he leaves on Tuesday. Where the park remains a funny anecdote. Where I archive this file and title it with the date and a word like April or Nice. That is the safe version. That is the version Sohee wants for me.

There is another version where he stays too long, tries too hard, breaks my heart because he has to return to his clean lines and his exacting family. I do not like either version.

I close my eyes. I think of his knee against mine. I think of him correcting the verb about my brother. Is. I prefer the story where we become evidence that reverence and laughter can live in one body without tearing it apart. That would be useful. That would be honest.

I sleep. Not quickly, but well.

Chapter Five: The Architecture of Quiet

Edward

Morning arrives not as a demand, but as a contract I finally want to read closely.

I rise before the alarm, stepping out of the tangle of sheets in a room that smells of three other men, damp towels, and the fading scent of last night's roasted chestnuts. The city outside is already revised: shopkeepers are unrolling the day with the metal clack-clack-clack of security shutters; a cyclist weaves through traffic transporting a square tower of cardboard boxes taller than his own decision-making; an auntie swipes the sidewalk with a straw broom that sounds like it has something encouraging to say to the concrete.

Our room is a chorus of four different snores and one long sigh from Michael, who is likely dreaming of a world where calories don't count. I spare them my piety. I grab my toiletry bag and step into the hall.

It is quiet here. The hostel hums with the low-voltage vibration of a refrigerator and the distant sound of water running in pipes. I lean my forehead against the cool window glass at the end of the corridor. I pray, but not the prayers of my childhood—rote, structured, filed in triplicate for God's review. Thank you for the kind light, I whisper, watching the sun hit the aluminum roofs across the alley. Thank you for the lesson that didn't announce itself as one. Help me walk through today like it deserves me.

Breakfast is a study in efficiency and joy. We crowd into a convenience store—the bells chiming a digital welcome—and buy onigiri triangles wrapped in seaweed that snaps when you bite it, and cans of coffee that are too sweet but somehow perfect.

We eat standing on the corner, watching the Seoul morning rush. "So," Michael says, brushing a crumb of rice from his chin. "When is the benediction scheduled, Reverend? Did the Phallic Park require a formal exorcism?"

I look at him. A week ago, I would have stiffened. I would have offered a dry retort about propriety. Today, I just roll my eyes and point to the handwritten sign in the hostel lobby visible through the glass doors. "The world can wait, Michael," I say. He blinks, surprised by the lack of defense, then laughs—a loud, barking sound that makes a passing businessman jump. "I am putting the world on notice," he declares. "Edward Gray has gone rogue."

We keep the itinerary simple. We split up. The boys want to hunt for knock-off sneakers in Dongdaemun. I want something else, though I'm not sure what until Jennie texts me. Market? she asks. Yes, I reply.

We meet at Gwangjang Market. If the hostel was quiet, this is the opposite. It is a cathedral of appetite. Steam rises in thick, savory clouds from stalls selling mung bean pancakes; vats of red tteokbokki bubble like molten lava; mountains of bibimbap ingredients are stacked with the precision of jewels. It is loud, chaotic, and smells of sesame oil and frying batter.

I watch Jennie move through it. She doesn't fight the crowd; she flows with it. She stops at a stall, exchanging quick, rhythmic Korean with a vendor who looks like she has been frying pancakes since the Joseon dynasty. There is a competence to Jennie that I envy. In the quiet spaces, she offers respect. Here, where money changes hands, she offers humor. The vendor laughs at something Jennie says—a sharp, cackling sound—and slips an extra tangerine into Jennie's bag. "What did you say?" I ask as we walk away, peeling the fruit. "I told her she looked too young to be running a stall, and she told me I looked too skinny to be happy." "And the tangerine?" "A bribe," she smiles, handing me a segment. "To fix my happiness."

We sit on a bench near the Cheonggyecheon stream to eat. The noise of the market is a dull roar above us, but down here, by the water, it is peaceful. She pulls out her phone. "Checking in?" I ask. "Sohee," she says. "She worries." She types something rapidly. A moment later, her phone lights up with a response. She tilts the screen toward me so I can see. It is a string of emojis: a knife, a bomb, a heart, a knife. "Translation?" I ask, raising an eyebrow. "Be safe. Be smart.

Be loved. Or I will cut him." I laugh, but I experience the odd sensation of wanting to be worthy of a stranger's knives. It feels good to know she is guarded, that she is precious to someone other than me. It makes my own growing care for her feel validated.

By late afternoon, the shadows decide to lengthen, stretching across the city like yawning cats. We return—just the two of us—to the coast of the Han River. It isn't the ocean, but it has a similar temperament at this hour: fair, unsentimental, present. We find a concrete overlook where the city noise is swallowed by the wind. Below us, the gray water lifts itself and sets itself down again like a disciplined breath.

I sit on the ledge, legs dangling, watching a ferry cut a white line through the water. "I could live by water," I say, surprising myself. I have always lived in brick and ivy. "Why?" she asks. "If it didn't insist on reminding you it cannot be managed. It feels… honest." "That's why some of us live by it," she says, pulling her knees to her chest. "It keeps your pride on a leash. You can't negotiate with a tide, Edward."

I laugh. "My pride has an opinion about leashes. It usually chews through them." She looks at me, her eyes dark and serious. "So does mine. I feed it, and then I send it to its room."

We talk about ordinary things, but in the growing twilight, they feel heavy with import. She tells me about her class schedule, about the smell of turpentine that clings to her clothes. She tells me about her father. "He says he hates fish," she says, looking at the water. "He complains about the smell, about the bones. And then my mother cooks it, and he eats it like a man in a contest. He picks the bones clean." "Why does he complain?" "Because complaining is how he says he worries about the cost," she says gently. "And eating it is how he says he loves her effort."

I nod, understanding that language perfectly. "My mother," I offer, "has this habit. Before a difficult day—a trial for my father, or an exam for me—she puts her hand right here." I touch my own cheek. "She holds it for three seconds. She doesn't say anything. It's like she's pressing a button for courage." "Does it work?" "I used to think it was annoying," I admit. "Now… I think I'd fail without it."

35

We are quiet for a long time. We talk about extraordinary things as if they were ordinary, because that is the only way to let them into a life without breaking the furniture. We talk about whether grief educates you or simply exhausts you. We talk about whether love should be allowed to ask for more than you have learned to give.

She does not tell me everything about her brother. I can feel the edges of that story, sharp and jagged, but she keeps them covered. I do not tell her everything about the gulfs around my family table— the nights when an argument is won by my father, and the silence that follows is so loud it rings in your ears. We are careful with each other. But not the way I used to be—careful out of fear of making a mistake. We are careful like carpenters, handling expensive wood, building something that does not collapse under the first strong wind.

"Tomorrow," I say finally, checking the time on my phone. The screen glows harsh in the dusk. "The boys want to try karaoke. They believe in proving their citizenship by volume. Michael has threatened to sing Journey." "You will sing?" "I will attempt civility," I say. "Which is a kind of music, if you listen hard enough."

She smiles, a slow expression that starts in her eyes. I find I want to protect that smile from needless explanations. I want to stand between it and the cynicism of the world. "I'll meet you after," she says. Then, as if revising the contract to give me an out: "If you want. There's a bookstore in Hongdae with a cat who acts like security. It's open late." "I want," I say. It is the truest line I've spoken in a while. It is a sentence without a clause, without a condition. I want.

We stand. The evening is filing itself by color—indigo, violet, charcoal. As we walk back toward the subway station, our shoulders brush. She asks the question the day has earned. "What did you decide?" she says. "About what?" "The park. The photos. The laughter."

I stop walking. I think about the wooden statue. I think about the shock of it, and then the strange, settling peace of realizing that the world is weirder and messier than my father's law firm allows. "I decided my discomfort doesn't get to be the judge," I answer. "And that laughter isn't the enemy of reverence if it remembers to bow."

She studies me for a heartbeat as if checking the fit of a new coat. "Good," she says. "That's how you don't get eaten by shame, Edward."

Back in the neighborhood of the hostel, we meet up with the boys. They are loud, carrying bags of cheap socks and plastic toys, vibrating with the energy of the city. We stop by Paris Baguette. It has become a liturgy. Rituals are reasons to stay human. We buy the cream roll we've adopted as our mascot and a croissant whose layers argue in favor of restraint. Michael insists we conduct a blind taste test against our first-day memories. Lorenzo records the proceedings on his phone like a documentary filmmaker—but a cheerful one, the kind that believes the thesis of the universe is joy.

Jennie and I share a small round table by the window while the verdict is debated and revised by the boys. She tears off a quiet piece of the croissant. The flakes rain down on the paper napkin. She passes it to me. "Evidence," she says. I chew. I consider. I taste the butter, the air, the sweetness. "Less sugar today," I say, meeting her eyes. "More intention." "See?" she says, leaning back. "You're fluent now."

Later, in the hostel common room, the others have gone to bed. The light has learned how to be warm without being dim. The kettle performs its small opera in the corner, boiling water for no one. I sit at the scratched wooden table. I have a notebook open. I do this sometimes—write testimony to the day, so I don't lose the evidence. I write about the tangerine. I write about the knives. I end up writing a line I didn't plan: Stand in front of it before you decide. I underline it once. It looks like something I want to remember even when I am tempted to forget. It looks like a rule for a life I haven't started living yet.

Jennie comes down the stairs. She is wearing oversized sweatpants and a t-shirt, her hair loose. She looks softer, younger. "Heading up?" she asks. "In a minute." She walks over to the table. She doesn't look at what I'm writing. She respects the boundaries of the page. She touches my sleeve. It is a touch so light it refuses to be misread. It is not an accident. "Edward," she says. The sound of my name in her mouth is a map I would follow anywhere. It sounds different than when my father says it. When he says it, it sounds like an obligation. When she says it, it sounds like an invitation. "Yes?" "Thank you for not being a joke," she says.

I look at her. I know what she means. She means thank you for not treating her country, her grief, or her park as a punchline. "Thank you for not letting me be one," I answer.

She smiles, withdraws her hand, and pads softly back up the stairs.

Sleep takes longer to negotiate this time. I lie in my narrow bunk. Above me, the ceiling is a landscape of shadows. My body wants rest; my mind wants to rehearse the day. Somewhere in the night, the building settles, as buildings do—groaning into the foundation. I think about how people settle, too—into better versions of themselves if they are lucky, or into smaller, tighter rooms if they are not. I intend better.

Years from now, I will still have the photograph she took—me unarmed, the sea making its argument behind my shoulder. Years from now, I will be a lawyer whose name appears in profiles with words like promising and unsentimental and popular, because I will learn how to speak in rooms that value victory over wonder. But I will also remember this: the day a stranger offered me lemon, and laughter beside the sea, and a way to stand in front of a complicated thing without turning it into a mask for my fear.

Tonight, though, I am only this: a man in a narrow bunk, in a city that knows how to hum, practicing out loud the kind of prayer that sounds like permission. Help me keep the room I found today, I whisper into the dark. Help me deserve the next one.

Chapter Six: Karaoke and Quiet Things

Edward

Night in Seoul does not fall; it rises.

It rises from the pavement in the form of steam vents and roasted street food. It rises from the subway stations in tides of students in uniforms and businessmen with loosened ties. And it rises, most aggressively, from the signage. The city, so gray and architectural by day, sheds its skin at dusk to reveal a second nervous system made entirely of neon.

We were in the Hongdae district, a neighborhood that seemed to operate on a frequency only dogs and twenty-year-olds could fully hear. The air vibrated. It wasn't just noise; it was a dense, layered polyphony of K-pop basslines thumping from cosmetic stores, the clatter of silverware from open-windowed barbecue joints, and the digital chime of arcade games.

"This way," Michael shouted, acting as our self-appointed Moses parting the Red Sea of revelers. "I found a place with a five-star rating on the sound system. If I'm going to butcher music, I want high fidelity."

We were herded into a building that looked like a narrow slice of glass and light. We took an elevator up four floors, the doors opening into a lobby that smelled of dried squid, stale beer, and disinfectant—the distinct, universal perfume of the noraebang.

This was not the open-mic karaoke of American dive bars, where you stand on a sticky stage and perform for strangers who are mostly ignoring you. This was intimate. Private. A series of soundproof honeycomb cells where groups of friends locked themselves away to exorcise their demons through amplification.

Our room looked like the inside of a neon heartbeat. The walls were mirrored, reflecting our confusion back at us infinitely. A disco ball spun lazily overhead, casting shards of pink, green, and electric blue light across the vinyl sofas. On the table sat two oversized

39

tambourines and a remote control that looked as complex as the dashboard of a fighter jet.

"Gentlemen," Michael announced, grabbing the wireless microphone as if it were a scepter. "Welcome to the Thunderdome."

Damion cued up the playlist, navigating the hangul menus with a surprising intuition. Lorenzo adjusted the echo settings—a knob labeled 'ECHO' that seemed to determine how much you sounded like you were singing from the bottom of a well.

And I—as usual—stood near the door, clutching a can of Korean beer, trying to look like a man who wasn't terrified of losing his dignity in two languages.

Michael went first. He chose a rock ballad, something anthemic and American. He didn't sing it; he attacked it. He threw his head back, veins bulging in his neck, screaming the chorus with a reckless sincerity that was almost frightening. On the screen behind the lyrics, a generic video played: a Korean woman walking sadly along a beach in a trench coat, looking at a pocket watch. It had absolutely nothing to do with the song, but the dissonance somehow made Michael's screaming more poignant.

When he finished, sweating and triumphant, he threw the mic to Lorenzo. "Top that," Michael panted.

Lorenzo didn't try to top the volume. He went for spectacle. He selected a high-energy K-pop track—something by Big Bang, I think—and attempted the choreography. He spun. He dipped. He missed beats. He looked ridiculous, flailing limbs against the strobe lights, but he was laughing so hard he could barely breathe.

Then Damion. The quiet one. He sat on the edge of the sofa, selected an old soul track, and crooned. It was low, unexpectedly smooth, and surprisingly tender. The echo effect caught his voice and wrapped it in velvet. We stopped drinking. We listened. For three minutes, the neon room felt like a jazz club.

Then, the inevitable silence. Three pairs of eyes turned to me. The remote was pushed across the sticky table. "Your turn, Counselor," Michael said. "I'll pass," I said, swirling my beer. "I'm observing. It's cultural research." "Bullshit," Lorenzo said. "The research requires participation. Pick a song, Gray. Or we pick for you. And if we pick, it's going to be Britney."

I looked at the remote. I looked at the mirrored walls. I saw myself—stiff posture, buttoned shirt, the eternal observer. I thought of Jennie at the park. Stand in front of it before you decide. She wasn't here, but the echo of her challenge was.

I picked a song. Something safe. Something English. "My Way." A cliché. The intro started—swelling strings and synthesized horns. I stood up. My hands were sweating against the plastic casing of the microphone. I started to sing. Softly. Respectfully. Trying to hit the notes with mathematical precision. "And now, the end is near…"

"Boooo!" Michael yelled immediately, throwing a piece of popcorn at me. "Boring! You sound like a eulogy! Wake up, Gray!" "Give it some chest!" Lorenzo shouted, shaking the tambourine aggressively.

I looked at the screen. The generic video had changed. Now it was a Korean man running through rain, crying, slamming his fist against a brick wall. It was melodrama. It was excessive. And suddenly, I understood.

This wasn't about pitch. It wasn't about talent. The entire city of Seoul—with its rigid social hierarchies, its intense academic pressure, its long work hours—came into these rooms not to sing, but to scream. It was about Han—that untranslatable Korean concept of sorrow, resentment, and the release of the soul. You didn't sing to sound good. You sang to let the pressure out of the valve so the machine didn't explode.

I looked at the lyrics. I did it my way. I thought of my father's email. I thought of the suit waiting for me in Boston. I thought of the terrifying, exhilarating feeling of falling in love with a girl who lived 7,000 miles away.

I closed my eyes. I stopped trying to sing. I started to shout. I missed the key. I cracked on the high note. I gestured wildly with my free hand, mimicking the man in the rain video. "FOR WHAT IS A MAN, WHAT HAS HE GOT?" I bellowed, my voice cracking, the echo reverberating in my own skull.

Michael cheered. Damion banged the table. Lorenzo fell off the sofa laughing. And something happened: I laughed too. mid-lyric. I felt a physical loosening in my chest, as if a corset I hadn't known I was wearing had been unlaced. I stopped worrying about the verdict of the room and started caring about the vibration in my throat.

I finished the song breathless, red-faced, and unmoored. "You sounded terrible," Michael said, handing me a beer. "It was beautiful."

After two hours of collective self-humiliation disguised as male bonding, the room felt too small. The air was used up. "I have to go," I told them, checking my phone. It was nearing 10:00 p.m. "I'm meeting Jennie." "Go," Damion said, slumped happily against the cushions. "Tell her you're a rock star."

I stepped out of the building and the silence of the street—relative to the noraebang—hit me like a cold towel. My ears were ringing. I walked toward the bookstore she had mentioned. The walk took me through the heart of the district. I moved through the crowds, feeling different. Lighter. Unarmed.

I passed a movie theater. The posters were glossy and dramatic. A thriller about a detective with a haunted past. A romance about lovers separated by time. I stopped for a second to look at them. Korean cinema was everywhere now—even in Boston, the arthouse theaters played Oldboy and Parasite. There was a specific texture to their storytelling—a willingness to mix extreme violence with extreme tenderness. They didn't shy away from the grotesque or the heartbreaking. They put it all in the frame. Just like the park. Just like the karaoke room. Why is my culture so afraid of the mess? I wondered. Why do we hide everything behind a suit?

I turned down a quieter alleyway, the neon fading into the softer glow of streetlamps. The bookstore was tucked between a noodle shop and a darkened florist. It had a wooden sign, hand-painted. A cat guarded the doorway. It was a massive, orange tabby with a notched ear, sitting on the welcome mat like a disgruntled security guard. "Excuse me," I whispered to the cat. It flicked its tail, judged me, and found me acceptable enough to let pass.

Inside, the air smelled of paper, vanilla, and dust. It was a library silence—heavy, respectful, filled with the presence of thousands of minds resting on shelves. Jennie was waiting in one of the narrow aisles near the back. She was holding a book, her head bent, her hair loose around her shoulders. She wore a long cardigan that looked like it belonged to a grandfather. She looked up when the floorboards creaked under my feet. When she smiled, the day rearranged itself. The noise of the karaoke room vanished.

"You survived?" she asked, her voice a whisper that carried easily in the quiet. "Barely," I said. "My ears are ringing. My throat hurts. I think I ruined Frank Sinatra for three of my best friends." She laughed softly. "That is the point. If your throat doesn't hurt, you didn't do it right." "I learned that," I said. "It's about the scream." "It's about the Han," she corrected gently. "The release."

She handed me the book she was holding. It was a slim volume of translated poetry. "This helps," she said. "To settle the blood." I opened it to the first page. I read the lines aloud, my voice raspy from the singing. "The wind blows. / The wind blows through the empty fields of my heart." The sound felt too loud in the small aisle.

Jennie picked up another book—a collection of essays on photography and memory. She began to read a passage, her voice overlapping with the echo of mine. "To photograph is to hold one's breath, when all faculties converge to capture fleeting reality."

We moved through the store slowly, stopping whenever a title invited conversation. It was a different kind of music than the noraebang, but it was music nonetheless. We stopped in the film section. I pulled out a book on Korean New Wave cinema. "I saw the posters outside," I said. "The movies here… they're intense. Operatic." "We like big emotions," Jennie said, tracing the spine of a book about the director Bong Joon-ho. "In America, I think you like resolutions. You like the hero to win. You like the case to be closed." "And here?" "Here, we know that sometimes the detective doesn't catch the killer," she said. "Or the lovers don't end up together. But the beauty is in how they tried. The beauty is in the suffering."

I looked at her. "That sounds painful." "It is," she said. "But it's true. I prefer truth to comfort." "I'm learning to," I said. "But my instinct is still to find the exit strategy. To fix the problem." "You like structure," she said. "You like the law because it promises an answer." "I do." "And you're afraid of losing it," she added, not unkindly. I considered that. She wasn't wrong. "I've been raised to feel responsible for my choices," I told her, the confession slipping out easier in the quiet of the books. "In a way that sometimes makes me choose caution over desire. I measure the risk of everything. Even this." "This?" "Being here. With you. It's high risk, Jennie."

She listened with her whole attention, the way she looked at the sculptures in the park: as if trying to understand the intention before the shape. "High risk," she repeated. "And the reward?" "I don't know yet," I said. "That's the terrifying part."

We stopped near the window display. The orange cat brushed past our ankles in a show of reluctant acceptance, weaving a figure-eight between my jeans and her leggings. "Do you ever wish you were different?" she asked suddenly. "Different how?" "Less careful. Less… defended. More like your friend Michael." I thought about Michael screaming into the microphone. I thought about my father buttoning his suit jacket. "Sometimes," I answered honestly. "Sometimes I don't know where careful ends and fear begins. I think I use the word 'prudence' to hide the word 'cowardice.'"

She nodded, as if she'd suspected that. "You aren't a coward, Edward," she said. "Cowards don't come to the bookstore after the party. Cowards stay in the noise."

She looked up at me. The streetlamp outside hummed softly, casting a warm, amber glow through the glass. Her face was tilted up, open, expectant. The air between us charged with a sudden, static electricity. The night tilted toward a kiss. It would have been easy. It would have been inevitable. The setting was perfect. The mood was right. I wanted to. God, I wanted to. I wanted to bury my hands in her hair and erase the distance.

But I stepped back. Just slightly. Just an inch. Just enough to steady the world. It wasn't rejection. It was the opposite. It was weight. I didn't want to kiss her casually. I didn't want it to be a vacation fling in a bookstore. I wanted it to mean something, and meaning required patience.

She didn't look offended. She looked like she understood exactly what was happening inside me, even if I barely did. "Not yet," I murmured, my voice thick. She smiled once, gently. A smile that forgave me and challenged me at the same time. "Not yet is still a beginning," she said.

We walked back through the streets that glowed like memory. The frenetic energy of Hongdae had calmed. The streets were quieter now, alive with small, intimate stories. We passed couples sharing tteokbokki on street corners, steam rising between them. We passed students in uniform heading home from late-night cram schools, looking exhausted but resilient. We passed an old man selling roasted chestnuts under a yellow bulb, the smoke curling up into the night.

I saw the city differently now. I didn't just see the neon and the architecture. I saw the narrative. I saw the Han. I saw the effort it took to live here, to love here, to strive here.

At the hostel entrance, I paused. The "World Can Wait" sign was visible through the glass. "Thank you," I said. "For what?" "For… today. For the poetry. For letting me be ridiculous in the karaoke room. And for not treating me like I was broken because I stepped back."

She touched my arm lightly. Her hand was warm through my shirt. "You weren't ridiculous," she said. "And you're not broken, Edward. You're just learning a new language." "Korean?" I joked weakly. She shook her head. Her eyes were dark and serious. "Living," she said. "You're learning that you don't have to solve the case to enjoy the mystery."

I didn't sleep right away that night. I lay in my bunk, listening to Michael snore, listening to the city hum outside the window. I felt a strange vibration in my chest—the phantom echo of the song I had shouted. I had crossed a small, important threshold. The kind that wasn't loud or dramatic. It was the quiet realization that I could step out of the suit, if only for a few hours.

As I drifted to sleep, I thought of her voice layered over the poetry. I thought of her eyes reflecting the bookstore lamplight. I thought of the almost-kiss, and how the restraint made it feel more intimate than anything that had actually happened. I prayed—not for clarity, not for a verdict, but for room. Room to be messy. Room to scream. Room to wait. For the first time in my life, that felt like enough.

Chapter Seven: Guardrails

Jennie

The restaurant where I meet Sohee is the kind of place that looks accidental from the outside—just a sliding glass door smudged with fingerprints and a narrow, flickering neon sign that simply reads Noodles. But inside, it is warm and stubbornly alive.

It smells of Anchovy broth, wet umbrellas, and the specific, fermented heat of gochujang. The tables are scarred wooden squares, small enough to force conversation, crowded enough that your elbows inevitably brush against your neighbor's. The steam from the open kitchen rises in thick, savory clouds, settling into your hair and softening the hard edges of the Seoul winter outside.

The ajumma behind the counter—a woman with permed hair and eyes that have seen every variation of heartbreak this city has to offer—nods at me as I enter. She knows if you've had a difficult week before you even sit down. Today, she just hands me a menu without a word, which I take as a good sign.

Sohee arrives exactly on time, shaking her umbrella with the precision of a woman prepared to fight.

She is wearing a trench coat that costs more than my tuition and lipstick the color of a warning sign. She slides into the seat opposite me, flicks her damp hair off her cheek, and gets straight to the point.

"So," she says, snapping her wooden chopsticks apart with a sharp crack. "Tell me about your American problem."

I sigh, unwrapping my own spoon. "He's not a problem."

"That's what they all say," Sohee counters, picking up a pickled radish. "That's what Min-ji said before the French guy moved back to Lyon. That's what Hannah said before the exchange student ghosted her. It's the preamble to crying in a subway station, Jennie."

"Sohee—"

She leans in, her dark eyes narrowing. "Okay. Fine. Defend him. Start. What's he like?"

I stir my kal-guksu, watching the steam rise, buying myself a moment. How do I explain Edward to Sohee? Sohee, who dates architects and tech consultants, men with five-year plans and pristine apartments in Gangnam.

"Careful," I say finally.

Sohee pauses, a noodle halfway to her mouth. "Careful like polite? Or careful like emotionally constipated?"

"A bit of both," I admit. "But… intentional. He doesn't speak just to fill the silence. He watches things. He listens."

"He listens," she repeats flatly.

"Yes. He doesn't pretend to understand things he doesn't. He asks. And he remembers. He's… kind."

Sohee chews slowly, her gaze dissecting my face. For a moment, her expression softens. She loves me; I know that. She has been my guardrail since we were fifteen, steering me away from bad haircuts and worse men. But the softness doesn't last.

"Jennie," she says, her voice dropping an octave. "Men like him come to Seoul all the time. They treat this city like a theme park. They fall in love with the food, or the nightlife, or the novelty of a girl who shows them the 'real' Korea. And then—poof." She makes a gesture with her hand like a magician vanishing a coin. "The visa expires. The job ends. The novelty wears off. I'm not saying he's a bad person. I'm saying he has options. He has a return ticket. You don't."

I've known her long enough to hear the fear beneath the sarcasm. She isn't attacking him; she's shielding me.

"He's not like that," I say quietly. "He feels… heavy. Like he's carrying things. He's not here for a party."

"So far," she counters. "But you're the one who has to stay. You're the one whose life doesn't fly home to comfort when things get hard."

I push my bowl away, my appetite suddenly dampened. "I'm not stupid, Sohee. I know the logistics."

"I didn't say you were stupid. You're brilliant." She reaches across the table, her manicured fingers squeezing my wrist. "I said you're romantic. And romantics are the ones who bleed the most."

That lands. I feel my throat tighten.

"I just don't want you hurt," she whispers. "Again."

The word again hovers between us, suspended in the steam. It summons old ghosts. Old wounds. The year after my brother died. The year I stopped painting. The year I tried to love a man who was just as broken as I was, hoping two shattered things could make a whole.

"I'm keeping my guard up," I promise.

Sohee releases my wrist and picks up her spoon. "Good. Keep it high. Concrete walls. Barbed wire. The works."

After lunch, I take the express bus alone to Gangneung.

It's been too long. The city dissolves into the industrial gray of the outskirts, which eventually gives way to the mountains. The bus hums through long, dark tunnels and bursts out into valleys dusted with snow.

I press my forehead against the cold glass. Sohee's voice rattles in my head. He has a return ticket. It's true. Edward is temporary. By definition, he is a visitor. To fall for a visitor is to sign a contract with an expiration date. But when I close my eyes, I don't see a visa stamp. I see the way he looked at the wooden ducks at the museum. I see the way he hesitated before touching my hand. I see a loneliness that matches my own, frequency for frequency.

The bus descends toward the coast, and the smell of the air changes. It becomes briny, sharp, and cold.

My parents' house sits a few blocks from the sea, tucked into a neighborhood of low brick houses and blue tile roofs. The paint on the gate is fading, peeling in long strips that flutter in the wind, but it feels earned rather than neglected. It looks like a house that has weathered storms.

My mother answers the door before I can even knock. She is wiping her hands on her apron, her face flushed from the kitchen heat. Her eyes light up before she even fully registers my face, a reflex of pure, unadulterated welcome.

"You're thin," she says immediately, pulling me inside by the arm.

"I'm not, Eomma."

"Come inside, you're thin. Your face is all angles. Are you eating? Is the city starving you?"

The living room smells like sesame oil, roasted laver, and laundry soap—the scent of my entire childhood. It is a smell that instantly disarms me.

My father sits in his old leather recliner, the one with the crack in the armrest, staring at the television. The volume is muted. A news anchor is mouthing words about the economy.

On the small table beside him, a glass sits. It is half full. Or half empty. It depends on what kind of day he is having.

"Appa," I say softly.

He grunts in acknowledgment. His eyes flick my way for a second— slow, slightly glazed, but present. There is love in that second. I know there is. But there is also a vast, unbridgeable distance he no longer tries to disguise. He retreated into that chair three years ago, and he has rarely come out since.

"Jennie is here," my mother announces loudly, as if he is deaf rather than just checked out.

"I see her," he murmurs. He takes a sip from the glass.

I look away. It hurts less if I don't look.

My mother serves enough food for six people. Doenjang-jjigae bubbling in a stone pot, grilled mackerel, five different types of kimchi, steamed egg. I eat because refusing would be an insult. I eat because in this house, food is the only language we have left to say I love you and I'm sorry and please stay.

We talk about safe things. "How is school?" "It's good. Hard." "And the painting? The exhibition?" "It went well. I sold a piece." "Aigoo, my daughter is rich now," my mother laughs, placing a piece of fish on my rice. "Did you hear that, yeobo? She sold a painting."

My father nods at the television.

In the hallway, visible from where I sit, my brother's photograph hangs on the wall. It is the centerpiece of the shrine my mother keeps dusted and fresh. Jun-ho. He is smiling in the picture, ear-to-ear, wearing his university jacket, looking like he planned to take laughter to the Olympics. He looks immortal. That's the trick of photos. They lie. They freeze the moment before the fall.

I catch my father looking at the photo, then looking at his glass. This is why Sohee worries. This is why I have guardrails. Because I know what happens when you lose the person you love most. I know that sometimes, you don't survive it. My father is still breathing, but he didn't survive.

Later, while my father naps in the chair, I sit on the back wooden steps with my mother. The wind is picking up, rattling the persimmon tree in the yard. It carries the scent of the sea like an old story—salt and decay and vastness.

My mother peels an apple with a small knife, the skin coming off in one long, unbroken ribbon.

"You look tired, Jennie," she says, handing me a slice.

"I'm fine."

"Is it school?"

"No."

She waits. She continues to slice the apple, her rhythm steady. Chop. Slice. Offer.

"It's a boy," I admit.

She stops slicing. She nods, staring at the fruit, as if she had already guessed. Mothers have a terrifying radar for the shift in their daughters' gravity.

"Is he good?" she asks.

"Yes."

"Is he Korean?"

"No. American."

She pauses, the knife hovering. She looks at me then, her eyes sharp and clear. "Ah. An American."

"He's… smart. And gentle."

"And is he yours?" she asks.

The question catches me off guard. Is he yours? Not is he rich, or is he handsome. But is he yours? Does he belong to your life? Or is he just visiting it?

I swallow, tasting the tart apple. "I don't know yet."

My mother sighs, a sound that comes from deep in her chest. She places the knife down. "Then be careful," she says gently. "Even good men can break things without meaning to. They move differently than we do. They don't always see the glass on the floor."

I lean my head on her shoulder. She smells of jasmine tea and patience and the faint, lingering scent of bleach from cleaning a house that is too big for two people.

"I'm scared," I whisper.

"Good," she says, stroking my hair. "Fear keeps you awake. Just don't let it keep you from living. Your father… he let the fear win. Don't be like him."

I close my eyes. "I won't."

By the time I return to Seoul that night, the city feels sharper. Louder. The neon crosses of the churches, the blaring screens on the skyscrapers, the rush of the subway—it all feels aggressive after the quiet of Gangneung.

I walk back to my studio, the cold air biting at my cheeks. I think about Sohee's warning. He has a return ticket. I think about my mother's question. Is he yours? I think about my father's glass.

I check my phone. There is one message from Edward.

Made it back to the hostel. The city feels empty without you showing me where to look. Hope you're safe. Tell your family I said hello, even though they don't know me.

I stop walking. I stand in the middle of the sidewalk, people streaming around me like river water around a stone. The city feels empty without you. Tell your family I said hello.

He is thinking of me. But he is also thinking of them—the invisible people who made me. He is acknowledging the parts of my life he hasn't touched yet.

Something in that makes my chest ache—a sharp, sudden expanding of the heart that feels dangerous.

Sohee might be right. He might leave. He might break me. But there is a difference between fear and foresight. And there is a difference between liking someone—enjoying their company, their face, their attention—and letting yourself love them.

Liking is safe. Liking is standing on the shore. Loving is walking into the water, knowing the tide is strong enough to pull you under.

I look at the message again. I type back: I'm safe. They say hello back.

It's a lie. But it's also a hope. Tonight, I'm not sure which difference scares me more—the fear of him leaving, or the terrifying reality that I want him to stay.

Chapter Eight: The Distinction

Edward

I woke before the others the next morning. The hostel room was heavy with the smell of damp towels, stale beer, and the shared exhalations of three other men who were currently sleeping the sleep of the righteous—or at least, the unburdened. Sunlight fought its way through the thin yellow curtains, illuminating dust motes dancing in the stagnant air.

I lay there for a moment, staring at the cracked plaster of the ceiling, feeling the familiar weight of my own existence settle back onto my chest. For a few hours in my dreams, I had been formless. I had just been a guy in a city he didn't know.

Now, I was Edward Gray again. The son. The heir apparent. The future law student whose acceptance letters were already being drafted in the minds of the admissions boards my father dined with. I wasn't just a traveler; I was an investment that was about to mature. The firm—Gray, Miller & Associates—wasn't just a building on Congress Street; it was a mouth waiting to swallow me whole.

I rolled over and checked my phone. It was 7:00 a.m. There was a notification from Boston.

From: Charles Gray Subject: Fall Admissions Strategy / Henderson Lunch

My stomach tightened. It was a reflex, involuntary and pathetic—the Pavlovian response of a son raised to view affection as a transaction and silence as a reprimand. I opened the email, the screen glowing harsh and white in the dim room.

Edward,

I've arranged a lunch with Senior Partner Henderson for the Tuesday after your return. As you know, he sits on the alumni board for the law school. This is a formality, but a necessary one to ensure your placement is secured for the fall term.

Read the attached bio on his recent appellate victories. He appreciates deference and hates small talk. We are laying the groundwork for your 1L summer associate spot now. Do not be late.

CG

No "How is Korea?" No "Hope you are enjoying your last summer of freedom." Just a command and a PDF attachment.

The email wasn't just a schedule update; it was a reminder of the conveyor belt I was strapped to. Law school in the fall. The Law Review. The clerkship. The Junior Associate office. The Senior Partner office. The name on the door replacing his when he finally retired. The path was so paved, so perfectly manicured, that I felt like I had already lived it. The suit had been tailored, pressed, and laid out on the bed; all I had to do was stand still while they buttoned me into it.

I felt a sudden, desperate need for air. I felt like the walls of the hostel were the walls of the firm, closing in. I pulled on my jeans and a sweater, grabbing my coat as I stepped over Lorenzo's backpack on the floor. I slipped out into the hallway and down the stairs, bursting out the front door into the morning.

The air in Seoul isn't technically "fresh"—it carries the scent of diesel, spicy broth, and heated pavement—but somehow, it always feels awake. It feels urgent. And most importantly, it felt indifferent. The city didn't care who my father was. The street vendors didn't care about my LSAT scores. The wind didn't care about the legacy of the firm.

I stood on the sidewalk, breathing in the cold, trying to scrub the feeling of my father's expectations from my skin.

My phone buzzed in my hand. I flinched, expecting a follow-up email attaching a dress code for the lunch. It wasn't. It was Jennie.

Tea later? Same café?

The knot in my stomach loosened, replaced by a different kind of tension—something warmer, lighter, but equally terrifying. It was the tension of a variable I hadn't accounted for in the grand equation of my life. I typed Yes before my brain could draft a pros and cons list. Then, because I wanted to be honest, I added: I'm already awake. I'll meet you there at 10.

The café was a small, converted Hanok house in a quiet alleyway of Insadong, tucked away from the main thoroughfare of souvenir shops and galleries. It smelled of aged wood and citron—a sharp, clean scent that cleared the head. I arrived ten minutes early, but she was already there.

She was sitting by a window that looked out onto a small courtyard garden where a single pine tree twisted toward the sky. She wore a thick oversized sweater the color of oatmeal and a scarf draped in a way that made it seem like she'd invented elegance by accident. Her dark hair was pulled into a loose knot, strands escaping to frame her face. She wasn't looking at her phone. She was just looking at the garden, her expression serene and unreadable.

I watched her for a moment from the doorway. In Boston, people didn't just sit. They checked emails, they read the Wall Street Journal, they optimized their downtime to ensure maximum productivity. Jennie was just... being. It was a skill I realized I didn't possess.

She turned, sensing me. Her face broke into a smile—not the polite, closed-mouth smile of the debutantes I met at university mixers, but a real one. One that reached her eyes and stayed there.

"I guessed," she said as I approached the table. There were two steaming cups already waiting. "Guessed what?" I asked, sliding into the chair opposite her. "That you would be early. And that you look like someone who needs warmth."

I wrapped my hands around the ceramic cup. It was hot, grounding me in the present. "Long night?" she asked. "Restless morning," I corrected. "The hostel was... crowded. And the wifi was too strong." She studied me, her gaze lingering on the dark circles under my eyes, the tension in my jaw I hadn't realized I was holding. She didn't look away. "You're thinking about home," she stated. It wasn't a question.

I smiled weakly. "Am I that transparent?" "Only to me, perhaps." She took a sip of her tea. "Or maybe you just have a 'Boston face' on today." "What does a Boston face look like?" "Like you're trying to solve a math problem that has no answer."

I laughed, a short, dry sound that surprised me. "My father emailed. He wants to schedule a meeting with a senior partner at the firm the day after I land. He sent me homework. A merger brief to memorize before I've even sat for my first law school lecture." "On your vacation?" "My father doesn't believe in vacations. He believes in 'strategic pauses.'"

Jennie frowned, tracing the rim of her cup with a finger stained slightly with ink. "And how do you feel? About the meeting?" I looked down at the tea, watching a slice of dried citrus swirl in the amber liquid. "I feel…" I hesitated. I was trained to be articulate, to have an argument ready, but around her, words felt clumsy. "I feel like the script is written in permanent ink. And I'm just the actor hired to read the lines. If I miss a cue, the whole play falls apart."

"You can rewrite the script, Edward." "I can't. Not without burning down the theater. And my father owns the theater."

She nodded slowly. She didn't offer platitudes. She didn't say "Just follow your dreams!" like someone who didn't understand the weight of legacy or the crushing pressure of gratitude. She just acknowledged the difficulty of it. "That sounds heavy," she said softly.

We sat in silence for a while. It wasn't awkward. With Jennie, silence wasn't empty space; it was just a bridge between thoughts. I drank the tea—it was yujacha, sweet and citrusy—and felt the cold dread of the email begin to recede, pushed back by the steam and her quiet presence.

"May I ask you something?" she said suddenly. "Without you getting uncomfortable?" I set my cup down. "Probably not. I get uncomfortable easily. But try."

She looked me dead in the eye. The playful light was gone, replaced by a curiosity that felt intense, almost surgical. "Do you like me?"

I blinked. It was such a simple question. Juvenile, almost. The kind of note passed in a middle school classroom. Check Yes or No. But coming from her, with that unwavering gaze, it felt loaded with implications I couldn't parse. "Yes," I said immediately. "Of course I do."

"And do you love me?"

The air left my lungs. I inhaled too quickly, choking slightly on nothing. The sounds of the café—the milk steamer, the low murmur of other conversations—seemed to drop away, leaving only the beat of my own pulse in my ears.

She didn't flinch. She didn't look embarrassed for asking. "Edward," she said, leaning in, her voice dropping to a register that felt like a secret. "I'm not asking for a declaration. I'm not asking for a ring. I'm asking if you know the difference."

I looked down at my hands. They were trembling slightly. I clasped them together to stop it. In my world, the word love was a weapon. It was used to manipulate, to bind, to create obligation. If you loved this family, you would secure the clerkship. If you loved your future, you would attend the dinner. Or it was a contract—something you entered into after due diligence, confirming that the other party had the right pedigree, the right future, the right assets.

"In my family…" I started, my voice rough. "Love is a promise. It's a covenant. You don't use the word lightly. You measure it. You weigh it against the risk." "Like a transaction?" "Like a verdict."

"And in mine," she said softly, "love is what you choose even when circumstances don't cooperate. It's not the result of a calculation. It's the variable that ruins the math."

I looked up at her. She was terrified, I realized. Underneath the composure, underneath the artist's gaze, she was terrified I would say no. Or worse, that I would say yes and run away. "I don't want to say it and have it mean the wrong thing," I admitted. "I don't want to lie to you." "What would the wrong thing be?" "That I'm swept up," I said. "That I'm infatuated with the exoticism of the trip. That I'm rebelling against my father by finding the person least likely to impress a Senior Partner. Or that I'm acting like this is a movie, and once the credits roll, I'll go back to being a pragmatic lawyer."

She listened, absorbing every fear I had been too cowardly to name. "And the right thing?" she asked. "That I mean it. That I can live it. That I can be the person who deserves it."

Her expression softened. The tension in her shoulders dropped. "You overthink everything, Edward Gray." "It's my job. Or it will be." "You're not on the clock right now." She reached across the table. Her fingers brushed against my wrist, cool and light. "Don't think about forever. Don't think about the merger brief or the partner meeting. Just tell me how you feel right now. In this chair. With this tea."

I swallowed. I looked at her—the stray hair, the dark eyes, the kindness that radiated off her like heat. "I feel… drawn to you," I said quietly. "More than I expected. More than I've ever felt with anyone. It feels like gravity. Inevitable." "Okay." "And I'm afraid of that." "Why?" "Because if I love you," I whispered, saying the word like it was a secret code, "I'm not sure I know how to do it right. I'm not sure I can be the man you need me to be while I'm trying to be the man my father demands I be."

Jennie took my hand fully now. Her grip was surprisingly strong. "Then let me tell you something," she said. "Because you are smart, but you are stupid about this." I managed a weak smile. "Tell me."

"Liking someone is about comfort," she said. "It's about enjoying the way they make you feel. It's easy. It's passive. You like the tea because it's sweet. You like the weather because it's sunny." She squeezed my hand. "Loving someone is about willingness."

"Willingness to do what?" "To be uncomfortable," she said. "To change. To grow. Not just with them, but because of them. Liking is a feeling, Edward. Loving is a decision you keep making."

I sat with that. A decision. Not a verdict handed down by a judge. A choice I could make. A choice I could keep making, every morning, regardless of where I was. Even in Boston. Even in law school.

"You make it sound like work," I said. "The best kind," she replied. "The kind that builds something that lasts."

We held hands for several seconds over the table. I looked at our fingers intertwined—my pale, uncalloused hand against her smaller, paint-stained one. It looked like a contradiction. It looked like a mistake. It looked perfect.

She let go gently, not pulling away, just releasing me. "Come on," she said, standing up. "Let's walk. You need to get out of your head."

We walked out into the street, side by side. Insadong was waking up. Shop owners were rolling up metal shutters with a clatter that sounded like applause. The smell of street food—hotteok frying in oil and egg bread baking—was beginning to fill the air. Tourists were filtering in, cameras around their necks, looking for souvenirs to prove they had been somewhere.

Usually, crowds made me anxious. I liked order. I liked personal space. But today, with Jennie beside me, the chaos felt like background noise. I was hyper-aware of the space between our shoulders, the way our steps fell into a synchronized rhythm without us trying.

We reached a busy intersection near the Anguk station. The traffic roared past—buses, taxis, scooters weaving through the gaps. The crosswalk light was red. A crowd gathered around us, waiting. I looked at the people. Businessmen in suits checking their watches, already late for lives they didn't enjoy. Students laughing. Grandmothers pulling carts. Everyone going somewhere. Everyone with a destination.

I looked at Jennie. She was watching the light, her profile sharp against the gray city. She wasn't rushing. She was just waiting.

Loving is a decision.

My father's email was still in my pocket. The brief was waiting. The expectations were waiting. The life I had planned was waiting like that tailored suit, stiff and unyielding. But Jennie was here.

I took a breath. I reached out. I didn't look at her. I just reached down and took her hand.

Her fingers curled around mine instantly. She didn't turn to look at me, but I saw her shoulders relax. I heard her exhale, a soft sound lost to the traffic, but loud enough for me. It wasn't a dramatic gesture. No one else noticed. But for me, it was an earthquake.

Holding her hand in public, in the middle of the day, with no purpose other than to be connected—it broke every rule of efficiency I lived by. It served no strategic purpose. It secured no future asset. And it felt right.

The little green man on the signal flickered to life. The crowd surged forward. "Ready?" Jennie asked, looking up at me. Her eyes were bright, reflecting the city and something else—hope, maybe. Or just patience. I squeezed her hand. "Yes," I said. "I'm ready."

We stepped off the curb together. For the first time in my life, I wasn't walking toward a destination I had been assigned. I was just walking with her. And that, I realized, was the difference. Liking is watching the person walk. Loving is walking with them, even when you don't know where the road ends.

Chapter Nine: Fault Lines

Part I: The Interrogation

Jennie

The first time I bring Sohee to meet Edward, I regret it before we even sit down.

I chose the location carefully: a vinyl bar in Hongdae tucked into a basement, where the walls are lined with records and the lighting is forgiving. It's the kind of place that usually feels like a sanctuary, smelling of dust and whiskey. But tonight, with Sohee walking ahead of me in her sharp trench coat and heels that click like a countdown, it feels like a courtroom.

Edward is already there. He stands when we approach the table. He is wearing a button-down shirt that looks too crisp for a dive bar, sleeves rolled up to the elbows. He looks painfully American. He looks painfully handsome.

"So," Sohee says, ignoring his outstretched hand to slide into the booth. She flicks her hair off her shoulder, her eyes scanning him like a barcode reader. "You're the famous Edward."

He smiles, and I can see the tightness in the corners of his eyes. He knows he is being evaluated. "I'm not sure about famous," he says, his voice steady. "But I'm Edward. It's nice to meet you, Sohee."

She leans back, crossing her arms. "Jennie talks about you. A lot." I glare at her. She ignores it. She is my best friend, which means she is contractually obligated to be my bodyguard.

Edward handles her scrutiny with a grace that annoys me slightly. I want him to be messy. I want him to crack. Instead, he signals the server and waits for us to order before he speaks. "I've heard a lot about you, too," he says. "Jennie says you're the one who keeps her from drifting away."

Sohee narrows her eyes. "Someone has to. Artists like to float. They forget that rent is due and that men leave." The air at the table drops ten degrees. I kick Sohee under the table. Hard. "Edward is visiting,"

I say quickly, smiling a smile that feels like plastic. "He has a few days left."

"Right," Sohee says, picking up her drink. The ice clinks against the glass. "A few days. And then back to Boston. To the big law firm." Edward nods. He doesn't apologize for it, which I respect. "That's the plan." "And what happens to the girl you leave behind?" Sohee asks. She doesn't look at me; she looks dead at him.

I freeze. This is why I didn't want them to meet. Sohee voices the fears I lock in the closet. Edward puts his drink down. He looks at his hands—those pale, careful hands—and then lifts his gaze to meet hers. He doesn't defend himself. He doesn't offer a charming lie about how distance doesn't matter. "I don't know," he says honestly. "I'm trying to figure that out."

Sohee blinks. She expected a defense. She expected arrogance. She didn't expect him to admit he was lost. "You're trying," she repeats, skepticism dripping from the word. "I am. I know how it looks, Sohee. I know I'm the tourist. I know I'm the one with the return ticket. But I care about her."

"Care is cheap," she snaps. "Plane tickets are expensive. Heartbreak is expensive." "Sohee," I warn. "No, let him hear it," she says, turning on me. "Jennie, look at him. He's a suit. He's a life plan. He's everything you ran away from when you quit graphic design. He is a walking, talking spreadsheet."

It's harsh. It's cruel. And part of me—a treacherous, terrified part of me—nods. She's right. He is a spreadsheet. He is safety and structure and rules. He is the opposite of my chaotic, paint-stained life. If I let him in, he will tidy me up. Or worse, he will leave, and I will be left amidst the mess he made of my heart.

Edward listens. He absorbs the blow. "You're right," he says softly. "I am all of those things." Sohee pauses. "But," Edward continues, "I don't want to be just those things. Jennie… she makes me want to be something else. Something less tailored."

For a second, the noise of the bar fades—the jazz record spinning, the laughter from the next table. Sohee looks at him, really looks at him, searching for the lie. She doesn't find one. She sighs, a long, dramatic exhalation of smoke she isn't smoking. "You're annoying," she decides. Edward smiles, and this time it's real. "I've been told."

We finish our drinks in a truce, but the fault lines are visible. Sohee likes him—I can tell because she starts mocking his accent—but she doesn't trust him. And why should she? She is looking at the math. Three days left. One ocean. Two different worlds. The math says we crash.

We walk Sohee to the subway station. The night air is thick, promising rain. At the turnstile, she hugs me. It's a fierce, bone-crushing hug. "He's good," she whispers in my ear, her voice low so he can't hear. "That's the problem, Jennie. If he were an asshole, this would be easy. You'd cry for a week and move on." "I know," I whisper back. "Be careful," she says. "Good men break hearts the worst. Because they don't mean to."

She pulls back, gives Edward a curt nod, and disappears down the escalator. We stand there, the mechanical hum of the station beneath our feet. "She hates me," Edward says. "No," I say, taking his arm. "She's scared for me." "She should be," he says quietly. I look at him. His face is shadowed by the streetlamp. He looks devastated. "Come on," I say. "Let's go home."

Part II: The Fracture

Edward

The walk back to Jennie's apartment is quiet. Sohee's words are ringing in my ears like tinnitus. He is a walking, talking spreadsheet. She saw right through me. She saw the lawyer, the heir, the coward who has a flight booked for Tuesday morning. She saw the gap between who I want to be (the man holding Jennie's hand) and who I am (Charles Gray's son).

I feel like a fraud. I am walking next to this woman who sees colors I can't name, who lives with a bravery I can't fathom, and I am dragging her toward a cliff edge.

We reach her building. It's a low-rise in a quiet neighborhood, the kind with tangled electrical wires overhead and flower pots on every balcony. We climb the stairs to the roof. This is her sanctuary. There's a mismatched collection of plastic chairs, a drying rack for clothes, and a view of the Seoul skyline that looks like a circuit board of light.

She sits on a wide wooden bench and pats the space beside her. I sit. I leave a few inches of space between us. I feel like I shouldn't touch her. I feel like I'm contaminating her with my impending departure.

"Tell me what you're thinking," she says. Her voice is the only soft thing in this concrete city.

I rest my elbows on my knees, staring out at the Namsan Tower glowing in the distance. "I'm thinking that Sohee is smarter than I am." "Sohee is cynical." "Cynicism is just pattern recognition," I say. "She knows how this ends."

"Do you?" Jennie asks.

I turn to look at her. The wind picks up, blowing a strand of dark hair across her mouth. Without thinking, my hand moves. I tuck the hair behind her ear. My fingers brush the line of her jaw, and the contact sends a shock through me that nearly knocks the wind out of my lungs. I leave my hand there, cupping her face. Her skin is warm. Real.

"This is harder than I expected," I admit. "What is?" "Liking you," I say. The word feels inadequate. "Wanting you. And knowing that in seventy-two hours, I have to put on a suit and walk into a boardroom and pretend that I didn't leave my entire soul on a rooftop in Mapo-gu."

Jennie covers my hand with hers. Her eyes are large, dark pools reflecting the city lights. "Then don't pretend," she whispers.

"I have to go back, Jennie. You know that. My father… the firm… the tuition deposit…" I'm listing the bars of my cage, hoping she'll tell me they're made of paper. But we both know they're steel.

"I know you have to go," she says. "But you are here now."

"Is that enough?" I ask. "To just have 'now'? Isn't that cruel? To give ourselves this when we know it gets taken away?"

She moves closer. The inches between us vanish. I can smell her—citrus and paint and rain. "Edward," she says, "life isn't a contract. You don't get a guarantee clause. You just get the moments you choose to take."

My heart hammers against my ribs like a fist. I look at her lips. I look at the pulse beating in her throat. The armor I have worn my entire life—the carefulness, the reserve, the constant eye on the future—it cracks. It doesn't fall away gracefully; it shatters.

"I don't want this to end here," I choke out. "Then don't let it end yet," she says.

And then she kisses me. Or maybe I kiss her. I don't know. It happens like a collision. It isn't a polite kiss. It isn't the kind of kiss you give someone when you're checking the time. It is desperate. It is a conversation we've been having with our eyes for days, finally spoken aloud.

Her mouth is soft, yielding, but there is a hunger there that matches mine. My hands move to her waist, pulling her in until there is no air left between us. I feel the warmth of her body through her thin shirt, and the reality of her—the physical, undeniable weight of her—anchors me.

We break apart, gasping. "This is a bad idea," she whispers, her forehead resting against mine. Her eyes are closed. "I know," I say.

"We're going to get hurt." "Probably. Definitely." "I don't want you to stop," she says. "I can't stop," I confess.

Part III: Unarmed

Jennie

Sometimes the truth doesn't stop you. It just warns you. And sometimes, you look at the warning, acknowledge the danger, and choose the cliff anyway.

I take his hand and lead him down the stairs. My apartment is small. It is cluttered with canvases and books. It smells of turpentine and tea. It is not the pristine, curated world he comes from. But when he steps inside, he doesn't look at the mess. He looks at me.

He looks at me with a reverence that makes my knees weak. But it's not the distant reverence of a museum patron. It's the reverence of a man who has been starving and has just found a feast.

He closes the door and locks it. The sound of the deadbolt sliding home is final. He crosses the room in two strides. He cups my face again, his thumbs tracing my cheekbones, and kisses me deep, slow, and devastating. I feel his control dissolving. I feel the "Edward" that Sohee mocked—the rigid, careful lawyer—melting away under my hands.

His hands are shaking as he unbuttons his shirt. He is usually so precise, so composed, but now he is fumbling. I reach out and still his hands. I finish the buttons for him. When I push the shirt off his shoulders, I see the tension he carries there. The weight of his father's name. I press my lips to his collarbone, and I feel him shudder.

"Jennie," he breathes, my name sounding like a prayer.

We move to the bed. It is a narrow mattress on the floor, surrounded by my sketches. When we touch, skin against skin, the world outside ceases to exist. There is no Boston. There is no Seoul. There is no time zone. There is only the friction of our bodies and the heat rising between us.

I remember the statues at Haesindang Park. I remember how I told him that the park was about honesty—about the body having its own truth, stripped of pretense. This feels like that. It is impressive in its honesty.

He is careful at first, treating me like something fragile, something he is afraid to break. But I don't want careful. I want him. I wrap my legs around him, pulling him closer, deeper. "Don't hide," I whisper against his mouth. "Be here. All of you."

Something in him snaps. A groan tears from his throat, low and guttural. He stops holding back. He takes me entirely. His movements become urgent, driving, possessing. He touches me with a kind of desperate worship, his hands mapping every inch of me as if he is trying to memorize me by touch alone. As if he is trying to imprint this moment onto his skin so he can carry it back across the ocean.

I arc into him, meeting his rhythm. I forget to be guarded. I forget Sohee's warning. I forget that in three days, this bed will be empty. I am crying, I think. Just a little. Or maybe it's sweat. Or maybe it's just the sheer overwhelm of feeling someone else's soul pressing against your own.

When the release comes, it feels like falling. We collapse together, tangled in the sheets, limbs heavy and intertwined. The room is silent except for our ragged breathing. He buries his face in my neck. I run my fingers through his damp hair.

"Edward," I whisper. He tightens his arms around me. "I'm here," he says, his voice rough. "I'm right here."

But even as he says it, even as we lie there in the afterglow, safe in the dark, I can feel the ticking of the clock. I can feel the fault line beneath us widening. We have crossed a line. We are no longer tourists in each other's lives. We are inhabitants. And eviction day is coming.

Chapter Ten: Countdown

Edward

The last three days in Korea feel like standing in a doorway I'm not ready to walk through. The physics of time seem to have broken; hours stretch out in agonizing slowness when I am alone, yet evaporate the moment I am with her. Everything I do—eating a tangerine, tying my shoes, laughing at Lorenzo's terrible jokes—feels heavy with the significance of the "final time." It makes the air thick, like grief disguised as oxygen.

But before the slow unraveling of time, there is the message from my father.

It arrives on a Tuesday evening, just as the sun is setting over the Han River, turning the water into a sheet of hammered copper. My phone vibrates against the wooden table of the hostel common room. Lorenzo and Michael are arguing about the best way to pack souvenirs; Damion is reading a guidebook for his next destination. I am the only one whose trip is ending in a verdict.

The tone of the message is polite, formal, but edged with urgency— the kind of urgency my father usually reserves for legal verdicts or medical updates about distant relatives he is executor for.

From: Charles Gray

Subject: Urgent: Future Planning

Edward, call me when you have a moment. It is important we speak about your trajectory before you land.

"Trajectory." Not "life." Not "plans." A trajectory is something calculated. A trajectory is mathematical. It implies that if I deviate by even a degree, I will miss the target entirely.

I call him that evening from the hostel rooftop. The wind is sharp, carrying the scent of rain and frying oil from the street vendors below. Laundry flaps on the neighboring building like a frantic signal flag. I brace myself against the railing, looking out at the endless sprawl of Seoul—a city that has somehow, in two weeks, taught me more about being human than four years of Ivy League education.

He answers on the first ring. "Edward," he says. His voice is steady, but there is a grain to it—a roughness I haven't heard before. It sounds like static on a clear line. "Hi, Dad." "Are you well?" "Yes." "Enjoying the trip?" I hesitate. "Very much. It's… it's been different than I expected." "Travel is useful for that," he says, dismissing the sentiment. "It clears the cobwebs. But cobwebs are not the structure of the house, Edward. We need to look at the foundation."

He sighs lightly—relief tinged with calculation. "Listen, I want to talk about the fall. About law school."

There it is. The speech. The inevitable pivot to efficiency. "Dad, I haven't even left yet—" "I know you're having a formative experience," he interrupts gently. "But you've always been disciplined. Now is the time to leverage that discipline. I had lunch with Dean Halloway yesterday." My stomach drops. "You did?" "Yes. We discussed your potential placement on the Law Review. He remembers you fondly from the mixer. He expects great things. We all do."

He pauses. I hear something in the silence—a strain, a hitch, a breath that sounds heavier than it should. It's a wet sound, buried deep in his chest. "Are you okay?" I ask, frowning at the phone. "Fine," he answers too quickly. "Just tired. The Anderson case is dragging on. The discovery phase is a nightmare." A lie. Or at least, not the whole truth. My father doesn't get tired; he gets focused. He devours fatigue and turns it into billable hours.

He clears his throat, and the sound is harsh. "The firm needs new leadership in the next few years, Edward. I'm not going to be at the helm forever. I want you to be prepared. I want you focused when you return. You have the potential to take the practice further than I ever did. You have the temperament."

The temperament. He means the coldness. He means the ability to detach. He thinks I still have it. And maybe, to him, I do. He hasn't seen me dance. He hasn't seen me cry over a wooden statue.

"Dad… is something going on?" Another pause. This one longer. Weighted. "Nothing to concern yourself with," he says quietly. "Finish your trip. But come home ready. The suit I ordered for you—the charcoal bespoke one—should be ready for the Henderson lunch on Tuesday. It's serious. It fits the part."

The suit. The metaphor made literal. A second skin I am expected to zip myself into, covering up the person I became here. "I'll be there," I say. "I'll be ready." The call ends with his usual words— Take care of yourself, son—but they fall heavier than they ever have before.

I sit on the rooftop long after the line disconnects. Below me, the city breathes. I imagine Boston, gray and brick and silent. I feel the phantom weight of the charcoal suit on my shoulders, stiff and unyielding. It feels like armor. It feels like a cage.

Jennie

The next day, I decide we need noise. Edward is fading. I can see it. Since the phone call—which he told me about in brief, clipped sentences—he has been drifting away. He is physically present, but his eyes are fixed on a point three days in the future. He is already rehearsing the role of the lawyer.

I cannot let him leave like this. I cannot let his last memory of Seoul be the dread of Boston. "We are going to a concert," I announce when I meet him for lunch. Edward looks up from his coffee. He adjusts his glasses, looking terrified. "I don't know… I'm not really a concert person. I prefer… acoustic sets. In chairs. With assigned seating." "That's because you've only gone to concerts full of people who are afraid to sweat," I tease. "Come on. Don't say no before you try. It's Big Bang. You can't leave Korea without seeing a spectacle." "Big Bang?" "Trust me."

Two hours later, we are standing in the Olympic Gymnastics Arena. It is a cavernous space, filled with twenty thousand people. The air is vibrating before the music even starts. It smells of excitement and perfume and electricity. Edward holds the yellow crown-shaped light stick I gave him like it's a radioactive isotope. He holds it away from his body, staring at it with suspicion. "This feels like a cult," he whispers in my ear. "It is," I shout back over the roar of the crowd. "But it's a happy one. Just wave it when everyone else waves it."

The lights go down. The scream that rips through the arena is primal. It is the sound of pure, unadulterated joy. The music starts. It is loud—bass-thumping, chest-rattling loud. The performers explode onto the stage. Edward stands stiffly next to me. He is watching, analyzing. He is probably thinking about the fire exits and the structural integrity of the balcony.

But then, the song changes. It's faster. The beat is undeniable. I grab his hand. "Dance," I yell. "No," he mouths. "Just a little! No one is looking at you, Edward! Look at them! They're looking at the stage!" He looks around. He sees Lorenzo and Michael three rows down, jumping up and down like children. He sees Damion nodding his head. He sees twenty thousand strangers losing their minds.

And then, I see it happen. The stiffness in his shoulders drops. The "lawyer" melts away. He starts to move. At first, awkwardly. A little bob of the head. A shuffle of the feet. Then, he looks at me. I am laughing, waving my light, singing lyrics I barely hear. I am free. And he wants to join me.

He raises the yellow crown. He jumps. Lorenzo catches sight of him and yells, "GRAY'S DANCING! ALERT THE PRESS! THE STATUE HAS COME TO LIFE!" Edward laughs—a real, open-mouthed laugh that exposes his teeth and crinkles his eyes—and he lets go.

For two hours, he isn't Charles Gray's son. He isn't the future editor of the Law Review. He is just a boy in a room full of light, holding the hand of a girl he likes, letting the bass rewrite his heartbeat. It is a baptism by neon.

When the concert ends, we stumble out into the cool night air, ears ringing, bodies humming with adrenaline. He leans against a concrete pillar, catching his breath. His hair is messy. His shirt is untucked. He looks magnificent. "See?" I say, poking his chest. "You lived." "Barely," he mutters, but he grabs my hand and kisses the knuckles. "Thank you." "For what?" "For making me forget what day it is."

Edward

Later, back near her apartment, the adrenaline fades, leaving a soft, melancholy exhaustion in its wake. We stop at the rooftop again. We seem drawn to high places, maybe because they make the problems on the ground look smaller. This is where we shared our first kiss. Where the fault lines opened.

She sits on the edge of the roof, dangling her legs over the side. The city is a sea of lights below us. "All day," she says softly, "you've been fighting it." "Fighting what?" "The return."

I sit beside her. "I can't help it. It's like gravity. I can feel the pull of it. The emails. The expectations. The suit." "The suit," she repeats. "You talk about it like it's a straitjacket." "Sometimes it feels like one. It's a very expensive, very well-tailored straitjacket."

She turns to me. Her face is illuminated by the red glow of a neon sign nearby. "I need to ask you something," she says. My chest tightens. "What is it?" "When you left Haesindang Park… did it change you? Or was it just a funny story to tell your friends?"

I inhale sharply. The memory of the park—the phallic statues, the initial embarrassment, the eventual surrender to the humor and humanity of it—floods back. "Yes," I say. "It did change me." "How?"

"I think…" I pause, searching for the right words. I want to be precise. "I think it showed me that honesty and vulnerability aren't opposites. I grew up thinking that to be respected, you had to be armored. You had to cover up the messy parts of being human. But that park… it's all the messy parts. It's grief and sex and humor and superstition, all out in the open."

I look at her. "And then I met you. And you're the same. You don't hide. You showed me that connection can be strange and beautiful at once. That you can laugh at a penis statue and still find it sacred."

She smiles, a watery, sad smile. "That's exactly how it changed me too," she whispers. "I used to think my grief for my brother had to be this solemn, quiet thing. That I couldn't laugh anymore. But you… seeing you try to understand it… it made me feel like I could breathe again."

We sit together in silence. The countdown is ticking. Three days have become two. Two will become one. But in this moment, on this roof, we are infinite.

Chapter Eleven: The Longest Night

Edward

The day before I leave, the world feels strangely tender, as if the city itself is bruising under the weight of my departure. The light in Seoul is softer today, filtered through a thin, milky haze of clouds that hangs low over the Han River, trapping the humidity and the exhaust fumes in a suspended embrace. The usual aggressive noise of the city—the staccato jackhammers of never-ending construction, the whine of delivery scooters weaving through traffic, the K-pop blaring from storefront speakers—feels muffled. Distant. It is as if the city knows I am grieving it before I am even gone.

I wake up in the hostel before the alarm, pulled from a shallow, anxious sleep by the sound of a garbage truck reversing in the alleyway below. The room smells of stale beer, damp towels, and the specific, enclosed musk of four men sleeping in a small space.

I lie there for a moment, staring at the plywood slats of the bunk above me. This view has been my reality for three weeks. It felt temporary then. Now, it feels like a sanctuary I am being evicted from.

Across the room, Lorenzo is snoring, a rhythmic, wet sound. One of his arms hangs off the top bunk, his fingers twitching in sleep. Below him, Michael is buried under his duvet, a lump of refusal. Damion is sprawled on the adjacent bed, his mouth open, drool pooling on the pillow.

I look at them for a long, silent minute. Three weeks ago, I was one of them. I was just a guy named Ed from Boston, looking for cheap beer, good Korean BBQ, and a story to tell at parties to prove I was "cultured." I was loud. I was confident. I was singular.

Now, looking at their slack, untroubled faces, I feel a chasm opening up in the center of the room. They are going back to be the same people they were when they left Logan Airport. They will talk about the soju and the girls and the food. But I am going back as someone else entirely. I have been carved out.

I slide out of bed, careful not to creak the floorboards. I step over a pile of dirty laundry and retrieve my main suitcase from the corner. I begin to pack with a methodical, quiet violence. I fold the shirts I brought from Boston—the stiff polo shirts, the crisp Oxford button-downs my mother packed, the beige chinos. They look like costumes now. Clothes for a stranger. Clothes for a lawyer.

I zip the bag shut. The sound is like a zipper on a body bag. Final.

I sit on the edge of the mattress, my back to my friends. I pull out my phone. The screen is too bright in the dim room.

Mom: He's asking when you land. Please call as soon as you are through customs. Don't make him wait.

I stare at the text. The guilt is instantaneous, a sharp hook in my gut. My father isn't just a parent; he is an institution. And institutions do not like to be kept waiting. I delete the notification without replying. I cannot deal with the institution today. Today, I am still just a man.

I open a new message to Jennie. My thumbs hover over the glass.

Can we meet later? I want to spend the day with you. Just us. No museums. No itinerary. I just want to exist in the same space as you.

Jennie

I receive the text while I am standing in the entryway of my mother's apartment in Mapo-gu. I had come back just to grab my overnight bag—my toothbrush, a change of clothes, the heavy wool socks Edward likes because his feet get cold. I thought I could slip in and out while my mother was at the market.

But the moment I slide the electronic lock open and step into the genkan, I know I am trapped.

The air in the apartment is thick, heavy with the smell of scorched sesame oil and suffocating tension. My mother is sitting at the low kitchen table, her back rigid. Her hands are knotted together in her lap, knuckles white.

And across from her, peeling a tangerine with violent, precise movements, is Sohee.

Sohee looks up as I enter. Her eyes are sharp, glittering with a mix of triumph and disdain. She doesn't smile. She pulls a segment of the tangerine free and pops it into her mouth, chewing slowly.

"You're packing," Sohee says. It isn't a question. It's an accusation.

I drop my bag by the door, the thud echoing in the small space. "I'm going out, Eomma. I'll be back tomorrow."

"Tomorrow?" Sohee repeats, letting the word hang in the air like a curse. She turns to my mother, switching to rapid-fire Korean, her voice pitching up into that tone of faux-concern she uses when she wants to destroy someone socially. "Auntie, do you hear her? She is spending the night. With him. The day before he leaves the country."

My mother looks at me, her face pale. She looks small in her housecoat, diminished by the aggressive energy Sohee is projecting. "Jennie... is this true? Is he leaving tomorrow?"

"Yes, he is."

"And you are going to sleep with him?" Sohee interjects, standing up. She walks over to me, blocking the narrow hallway that leads to my bedroom. "Have you no pride, Jennie? He is checking out of his hotel, and he needs a warm place to put his body before he gets on the plane. You are just a convenience to him. A final amenity."

"Shut up, Sohee," I snap, my hands trembling. I try to step around her, but she moves to block me.

"I am trying to save you!" Sohee shouts, dropping the pretense of politeness. "I have been telling Auntie for weeks. This American, he is not here for culture. He is not here for you. He is on a... what do they call it? A gap year? A joyride."

She steps closer, invading my personal space. I can smell the citrus on her breath. She lowers her voice so only I can hear, though I know my mother is straining to listen.

"He is rich, Jennie. I looked him up. I Googled his name. His father's firm represents pharmaceutical companies and defense contractors. Do you think a boy like that brings a girl like you home to his mother? You are a souvenir. You are a story he will tell his friends in a bar in Boston to make himself sound interesting. 'Oh, the Korean girl? She was so wild. She was so easy.'"

The slap echoes in the small room before I even realize I've moved.

My hand stings. Sohee's cheek blooms red. She stares at me, stunned, hand flying to her face. My mother gasps, standing up and knocking over her chair. "Jennie!"

"Don't you ever speak about him like that," I whisper, my voice shaking with a rage I didn't know I possessed. It burns in my throat, hotter than the shame. "You don't know him. You see a passport. I see a person. You see money. I see the man who sat on a cliff and cried because he didn't know how to talk to his father."

"He is using you for sex!" Sohee screams back, tears of humiliation springing to her eyes. "He is leaving, Jennie! That is the only fact that matters! If he loved you, he would stay. If he respected you, he wouldn't ask you to spend his last night pretending this has a future!"

She turns to my mother, playing her final card. "Auntie, tell her. Tell her not to go. Tell her she is shaming the family by chasing a man who has already one foot out the door."

The room goes silent. The refrigerator hums. A car honks outside. I look at my mother. She looks at Sohee's red cheek, then at my clenched fists. She walks over to me, her slippers shuffling on the linoleum.

"He is leaving?" my mother asks quietly.

"Yes."

"And you know he is not coming back?"

"He says he will. But... I don't know."

My mother sighs. It is a sound of infinite weariness. She reaches out and tucks a loose strand of hair behind my ear. She looks at Sohee, who is waiting for the verdict.

"Sohee, go home," my mother says.

"But Auntie—"

"Go home," my mother says, her voice steel. "Jennie is my daughter. If she wants to make a mistake, it is her mistake to make. It is not your tragedy to narrate."

Sohee stares at us, her mouth open. She looks from me to my mother, realizing she has lost the high ground. She grabs her purse, scowls at me with pure venom, and storms out, slamming the door hard enough to rattle the framed photos on the wall.

The silence she leaves behind is heavy.

"You love him," my mother says. It is a statement.

"I think I do."

"Then go," she says, turning back to the kitchen to pick up the fallen chair. "But take the kimchi from the fridge. He looks too thin."

I grab my bag. I run out the door. My heart is hammering against my ribs, a mixture of adrenaline and fear. Sohee's words act like a slow poison in my blood—he will forget you, he is using you—and I need to see him. I need to see his face to burn the doubt away.

Edward

She waits for me by a small bakery near the university. She looks flushed, her breathing shallow, as if she has been running. When she sees me, she doesn't just smile; she grabs my hand like she's drowning.

"You okay?" I ask, feeling the tremor in her fingers.

"Let's just go," she says fiercely. "Let's go now."

We walk through Seoul without a map. We are drifting. We weave through the back alleys of Insadong, away from the tourist traps selling cheap masks. We find a stone wall covered in ivy and trace the lines of the mortar. We watch an old man painting calligraphy with water on the pavement, the characters evaporating almost as soon as he writes them.

We duck into a stationery shop to escape the wind. It is a quiet, narrow place that smells of paper, cedar, and old glue. The walls are lined with floor-to-ceiling shelves of notebooks, pens, and ink stones.

I touch the fountain pens, feeling the weight of the brass and the cold lacquer. "You like pens," she notes.

"I like tools that last," I say. "I like the idea that you can write a thousand words with one cartridge. I like that ink is permanent. It doesn't evaporate like the water on the pavement."

"What would you write?" she asks. Her voice is soft, lacking its usual teasing edge.

"Right now? A plea bargain with time."

She picks up a small, leather-bound notebook. It is dyed a deep, midnight blue, the leather soft and distressed. "Buy this," she says. "For law school. When you're sitting in those lectures, and you hate it, write something in here that isn't about the law. Write about the coffee. Write about the light hitting the Han River. Write about me."

I look at the book. It feels heavy, like a promise I'm not sure I can keep. "I will."

By mid-afternoon, the city feels too crowded. Every face I see reminds me that I am a foreigner, a temporary fixture. I need quiet. I need the origin of us.

"Let's take a train," I say. "Somewhere quiet."

She knows exactly where I mean.

Jennie

The train ride to Gangneung feels different this time. It's not an adventure. It's a pilgrimage.

Edward sits beside me, his thigh pressed against mine. He isn't reading a book. He isn't checking his phone. He is just watching the world go by outside the window—the gray industrial outskirts fading into rice paddies, then rising into the mountains.

At one point, the train slows, and he murmurs, "I wish I had more time. I wish I had met you a year ago. Or five years from now."

I don't say me too, because the tragedy of timing is boring. I just squeeze his hand. "We have now," I say. "Don't rob the present to pay the future."

When we arrive in Samcheok, the late afternoon light is turning gold. We walk the familiar path toward Haesindang Park. We don't go into the main exhibit. We stop short, climbing a small deer trail to the cliffs overlooking the water.

The sea greets us the way it always does: honestly. Indifferent to our heartbreak. The waves crash against the rocks, white foam dissolving into dark blue.

"I laughed at this place the first time," Edward says, looking at the distant shapes of the wooden carvings—the phalluses standing guard against the ocean. "I made jokes. I was so… American."

"You were embarrassed," I tease gently.

"I was closed," he corrects softly. "Not embarrassed. Closed. I thought I had to be. I thought being an adult meant being rigid. That if you weren't serious, you weren't safe."

He turns to me. The wind lifts his hair. He looks younger than he did when we met. Less guarded.

"Jennie… there's something I need to tell you."

My heart stills. I can feel the weight of his confession before it leaves his mouth.

"I think I'm starting to understand myself better. I thought… loving someone meant I had to be perfect first. That I had to have all the answers. That I had to be the finished product my father wants. That I had to present myself to you like a completed case file."

He pauses, his voice shaking. "But maybe loving someone means you get ready while you love them. Maybe it's messy. Maybe I'm not ready, but I love you anyway."

Tears prick my eyes. I think of Sohee's words. He is using you. I look at Edward's face—open, terrified, sincere. Sohee is wrong. This isn't a game. This is the realest thing either of us has ever felt.

"You don't have to have answers tonight," I say, taking his hand. "I never asked for the lawyer. I asked for the man."

"I want to show up for you," he says. "Fully."

He closes his eyes. When he opens them, the sun is dipping below the horizon. "I don't want to go back," he whispers. "I feel like I'm going back to a cage."

"Then leave the door unlocked," I say fiercely. "Don't let them lock you in, Edward. Keep a part of you here."

He leans in. Our lips meet with a softness that hurts. It is a kiss of desperation and promise. It tastes of salt air and finality. His hand slides into my hair, holding me like I might vanish if he lets go.

Later, we lie together on the flat rock, watching the stars emerge over the East Sea. The temperature drops, freezing the breath in our lungs, but neither of us moves. We share body heat. We share breath. We don't rush to the hotel. We don't rush to sex. We just lie there, defying every cynic in the world, existing in the liminal space between arrival and departure.

For the first time since receiving his father's email, Edward stops shaking. He is just here. And I pray to whatever gods live in this strange, holy, phallic park: Let him remember this.

Chapter Twelve: Departure

Jennie

The sun rises too quickly the next morning. It feels malicious. It enters the window of the hotel room like an eviction notice, slicing across the bedspread in a harsh, bright line.

I lie still for a moment, listening to Edward breathe. I memorize the rhythm of it. In an hour, that sound will be gone from my life.

I watch him pack. It is a terrible thing to watch. The folding of shirts. The winding of cords. The zipping of zippers. Each sound is a small door closing. He moves with a grim efficiency, the "Golden Boy" taking over the movements of the lover. He is putting on his armor.

We meet his friends outside the hostel later, where he has retrieved the rest of his things. Lorenzo, Damion, and Michael are there with their massive backpacks, looking unusually somber.

The dynamic is brittle. Lorenzo is bouncing on the balls of his feet, wearing sunglasses even though it is overcast, desperate to break the tension.

"So," Lorenzo says, clapping his hands together. "Last meal in Korea. Who wants Burger King? I saw one by gate 12. I need a Whopper. I need American cheese. I need to wash the taste of fermented cabbage out of my mouth."

"Read the room, Lorenzo," Michael says, his voice low. Lorenzo retorted, "she's with Edward over there, she probably isn't even listening to me, plus the sooner Edward realizes the better." Lorenzo continues and rolls his eyes, "I'm just saying. We're going home. It's time to pivot. Pivot back to reality." He looks at Edward. "Hey, man. Don't look so tragic. It was a hell of a trip."

Edward doesn't look up from the floor. "It was more than a trip."

"Sure, sure," Damion chimes in, adjusting his backpack straps. "It was an experience. But seriously, Ed. You're going to law school in the fall. You're going to be interning at your dad's firm. This?" He gestures vaguely between me and Edward, a dismissive wave of his hand. "This is the summer fling to end all summer flings. It's a great story. You'll tell your grandkids about the artist girl."

"It's not a story," Edward says, his voice sharp.

"Ed, come on," Lorenzo laughs, oblivious to the danger in Edward's tone. "It's geography. It's physics. You go back, you get busy, you meet some girl at a mixer who knows what a tort is. You'll forget about all this in a month. Two months, tops. It's how the brain works. Survival instinct. You purge the vacation data to make room for the work data."

I feel the blood drain from my face. It is an echo of Sohee's voice. He will forget you. He is using you.

Edward takes a step toward Lorenzo. His fists are clenched. "Shut up man, why do you always have to be such a jerk at times."

"I'm just being a friend!" Lorenzo says, putting his hands up in mock surrender. "I'm managing expectations! Better to rip the band-aid off now than—"

Michael steps in. He shoves Lorenzo hard in the chest, pushing him back. "Shut your mouth, Lorenzo. Seriously. Just stop talking."

Michael turns to Edward. He puts a hand on Edward's shoulder. Michael was the quiet one on the trip, the one who sketched in the margins of his guidebooks, the one who actually looked at the temples instead of just taking selfies.

"Don't listen to them," Michael says softly. "They're idiots. They think everything is disposable."

Edward looks at Michael, his eyes red-rimmed. "It feels like I'm cutting off a limb, Mike."

"I know," Michael says. "I can see it." He glances at me, offering a sad, respectful smile. "It's real, Ed. Just because it's ending doesn't mean it wasn't real. Don't let them cheapen it."

Edward exhales, a shuddering breath. He nods. He turns away from his friends, turning his back on their cynicism, and pulls me toward a quiet corner near the window, away from the staring eyes of travelers.

"I heard some of what Lorenzo said," I whisper.

"They're wrong," Edward says fiercely. "They don't know me. They don't know us."

We take the airport bus in silence. The city scrolls past the window—the bridges, the apartments, the river. I hate it all for continuing to function while my world is stopping. His hand grips mine the entire way, his thumb tracing the back of my knuckles, over and over, as if trying to memorize the bone structure.

Inside Incheon Airport, everything feels too loud. Too bright. The robots gliding by with their digital smiles, the announcements in three languages—it is all indifferent to the fact that my heart is breaking.

We find a spot near the security gate. He sets his bag down. He looks at me with an expression I can't read—part bravery, part terror.

"I need to ask you something," I say. "Anything."

"When you go home… when you put the suit on… are you going to disappear?" My voice trembles. "Are you going to become Charles Gray's son and forget about the guy who sat on the cliffs?"

He takes both my hands. His grip is tight, almost painful. "No," he says quickly. "I won't disappear. I promise."

"But will you stay?" I whisper. "Stay in whatever this is between us? Even when the ocean is in the way? Even when your father tells you it's impractical?"

He presses his forehead to mine. I can feel the heat of his skin. "I want to. I'm scared I won't know how to do it right. But I want to."

He pauses, pulling back slightly to look at me. His eyes are wet. "There's something else."

"What?"

"My father… he's not well." My breath catches. "He hasn't told me everything," Edward continues softly. "But he's hinted. And that phone call this morning… something in his voice. I think he's ill. Something serious. And he wants me home to take over. He's speeding up the timeline."

My eyes soften, filling with empathy and a new, colder fear. If his father is sick, the cage will be even harder to escape. Duty is a stronger chain than ambition. A son cannot abandon a dying father, even if the father is a tyrant.

"Edward… I'm so sorry., but don't assume the worst."

"I don't know what to do," he admits. "I don't want to leave you. But I can't ignore him. Not now."

"You shouldn't," I say firmly. "Family matters. Illness matters. Go to him. Be the good son."

"But so do you," he whispers. "You matter."

A final boarding call echoes over the speakers. Flight KE093 to Boston.

The sound is physical. It hits me in the chest. I look up at him, tears gathering but not falling. I will not cry until he is gone. I will not make this harder for him.

"Come back," I say.

"I will."

"Promise me you'll try."

"I promise."

And then, in the middle of that sterile airport, surrounded by strangers rolling suitcases, we kiss. It is not a movie kiss. It is messy and wet and frantic. It is the kiss of people who know that goodbye doesn't cancel love—it just challenges it to survive without air.

He pulls back. He memorizes my face. I memorize his.

"Go," I whisper. "I'll see you again."

"I'll be here."

He picks up his bag. He walks toward security. Each step looks heavy. He is walking away from the light and back into the shadow of his life. He stops at the glass partition. He turns back. I raise my hand. He nods once—a silent vow—and then he is gone.

Edward

Never has the sight of a plane seems so distant and unwelcoming. Normally airplanes smell of recycled air, not so pleasant coffee, and the varied mix of colognes/perfumes and deodorant. This instead felt like walking into a bad hallowed dark room.

I sit in seat 42A, pressing my forehead against the plastic window. Below me, Seoul is shrinking. The Han River is a silver thread. The mountains are wrinkles in the earth. Somewhere down there is a rooftop. Somewhere down there is a café with citron tea. Somewhere down there is Jennie, standing in an airport terminal, walking away alone.

The plane banks, turning East. I close my eyes. I feel the physical sensation of the distance growing, mile by mile. It feels like a rubber band stretching, tighter and tighter, until it snaps against my ribs.

I look to my right. Michael is already asleep, headphones on, mouth slightly open. Lorenzo and Damion are three rows ahead, laughing at an action movie. I am alone in the dark.

I reach into my pocket. I touch the leather notebook Jennie made me buy. Then, I reach into my bag and pull out the tablet. I open the email from my father again.

Except it isn't from my father. It was sent from his account, but the signature at the bottom is my mother's initials: M.G.

Subject: Updates.

It contains no official medical records. Just a scanned list of upcoming appointments. Neurology - Dr. Evans. Physical Therapy - 4pm. And a receipt for a pharmacy co-pay attached as a JPEG.

The lawyer in me wakes up. The part of my brain that hunts for the truth in the fine print, the part my father trained to be ruthless. I zoom in on the pharmacy receipt. It's blurry, scanned hastily, likely while he was asleep.

I can see the date—two days ago. And I can see the medication code. Rytary.

I frown. I don't recognize the name. I connect to the in-flight Wi-Fi. It costs twenty dollars and moves at the speed of a dial-up connection. I watch the loading bar crawl, my heart hammering in my chest against my ribs.

I type into the search bar: Rytary medication uses.

The page loads pixel by pixel.

Rytary (carbidopa and levodopa) is an extended-release combination medicine used to treat symptoms of Parkinson's disease, such as muscle stiffness, tremors, spasms, and poor muscle control.

Parkinson's.

I stare at the screen. The turbulence bumps the plane, shaking the tray table, but I don't feel it. The world has stopped.

I think back to Christmas dinner in Beacon Hill. The way he held his wine glass. There was a tremor. A tiny, rhythmic shaking of his right hand that rattled the stemware. He had set the glass down quickly, covering his hand with a linen napkin. I had thought he was just tired. I had thought he was stressed about the Anderson merger.

He knew. He knew then.

I search again: Parkinson's prognosis.

Progressive nervous system disorder... movement is affected... speech becomes soft or slurred... eventually requires full-time care.

My stomach drops. My father—the monolith, the man who speaks in thunder, the man who commands boardrooms with a glance—is going to lose his voice. He is going to lose his control.

Suddenly, everything makes sense. The pressure to come home immediately. The obsession with my "image." The way he pushed me onto the Lincoln campaign. He isn't just building a legacy; he is frantically trying to secure it before he becomes unable to run it. He is scared.

The realization hits me with the force of a physical blow. I am not just returning to a job. I am returning to be his hands. His voice. His proxy.

If I had stayed in Korea... if I had missed that flight... I wouldn't just be a disappointment. I would be a deserter. I would be abandoning a helpless man to his own decay.

The cage just locked. And I am holding the key, but I cannot turn it.

I look at the tablet screen until it blurs. A wave of complex, nauseating emotion washes over me. Anger that he hid it. Fear for his health. And a terrible, crushing realization of the potential trap I am walking into.

Did mom, mistakenly send this? Was this just preliminary research on a topic that she was doing and using dad's name as the subject? All these questions swirl in my thoughts. But ultimately if it's the worst-case scenario, I cannot leave him. Not now. Not while he is crumbling. I have to put the suit on. I have to become the man he needs, even if it kills the man I want to be.

I close the tablet. I look out at the clouds. We are over the ocean now. The in-between place.

I put my hand over the blue notebook in my pocket, holding onto the ghost of her warmth.

I won't disappear, I promised her.

But as I stare into the dark, watching the map on the screen trace our path toward Boston, I realize that to save my family, I might have to go deep undercover. I might have to bury Edward Gray so deep that even I can't find him.

I hope to God I wasn't lying.

Chapter Thirteen: The Unknown Knowns

I. The Return

Edward

The morning I return to Cambridge, the sky is flat and gray in a way that feels symbolic—an unspoken warning about the years ahead. My father picks me up from the airport in his black sedan. His hands are steady on the wheel, the radio tuned to NPR, the volume low enough that we're both pretending to listen to it instead of the thoughts crowding the space between us.

I keep seeing Seoul out the window. Instead of the brick facades of Beacon Hill, I see neon signs reflecting on wet pavement. Instead of the Charles River, I see the dark expanse of the Han. I hear Jennie's laugh carried across the rocky cliffs at Haesindang Park.

But here I am again. Back in the life I was raised for. Back in the suit.

"Classes start Monday," my father says as we merge onto the highway. It is a statement of fact, but it lands like the beginning of a mission brief. "Professor Lang has you on his roster already. I spoke to him at the club."

My stomach tightens at the name. Professor Lang is a legend at the law school. He is known for sharpening students until they either break or become something terrifyingly effective. He doesn't teach the law; he teaches how to weaponize it.

"Good," I say. But part of me wonders: Good for whom?

He glances at me, his eyes scanning my face for weakness, for jet lag, for hesitation. "You're ready," he decides. I should be. I should feel steady. Centered. Focused. But all I feel is the space Jennie occupies in my mind—alive, warm, impossible to ignore. It is a room in my house that I am trying to lock, but the door keeps swinging open.

II. The Machine

The First Class

Lang's lecture hall is colder than it should be. It is a tiered amphitheater of polished wood and silence. I take a seat near the front—not because I want attention, but because Lang's glare grows violent if you hide in the back. The room fills with the rustle of expensive notebooks, the clicking of pens, the palpable tension of ambition. First-year law students carry their competitiveness the way athletes carry muscle—visible, practiced, tremoring beneath the surface. They are all sharks who haven't smelled blood yet.

Lang enters. He is a small man with the presence of a giant. He carries a single stack of case briefs tucked under one arm and the weariness of a man who has taught too many students who weren't worth teaching. He arranges his papers. He scans the room. His eyes stop on me.

"Mr. Gray," he says. His voice slices through the ambient chatter like a gavel. "You're back." The room turns. A hundred heads swivel. A few students whisper. Gray? Charles Gray's son? Some glare. A handful look relieved—at least the spotlight isn't on them.

"Glad to see you didn't stay in Korea permanently," Lang adds dryly, opening a file. "I heard rumors you might defect for the art scene." I force a thin smile. "If only for the food, Professor." A few nervous laughs ripple through the room. Lang doesn't laugh. He never laughs. "Let's begin," he says sharply. "Hawkins v. McGee. Who can tell me the measure of damages?"

And just like that, I'm back in the machine.

Finding the Rhythm… and Losing It

The first weeks pass in a strange, hypnotic rhythm: Read. Analyze. Synthesize. Repeat.

I skim through case law faster than I ever did before Korea. Something about the time away made my mind sharper—like stepping outside my own life recalibrated the lens. I see the arguments before they are fully formed. I see the flaws in the logic like cracks in a windshield.

Lang notices immediately. "Gray," he barks during a discussion on torts. "Give us the rule." "Gray—interpret this statute." "Gray—

what is the underlying conflict here? Not the legal one. The human one."

At first, I'm flattered. Then I'm pressured. Then I'm exhausted. But brilliance becomes a shield—one I hide behind. If I am the best student in the room, no one asks me how I am feeling. If I am the "Gray heir," no one asks me why I stare out the window when it rains.

And behind that shield is the truth: I am not okay. Because no matter what I achieve here—the highest grade on the brief, the nod of approval from the Dean—a part of me feels like an amputee. I feel like I left a limb on a South Korean coastline, leaning into the warmth of a girl who smelled like citrus shampoo and sea air.

III. The Drift

Messages That Don't Align

Jennie messages me the second week: How was class?

I am in the library. It is midnight. I am surrounded by towers of books on contract law. I respond within minutes: Good. Intense. Lang is Lang. He ate a student alive today for citing the wrong precedent.

She sends a laughing emoji. But then her message sits there, waiting for mine to continue. Waiting for warmth, for details, for the pieces of myself I used to give so easily in Seoul. I type: Miss you. Delete.

Wish you were here. The coffee is terrible. Delete.

I'm tired. I feel like a fraud. Delete.

I settle on something safer. Something a lawyer would send. What about you? How's the studio? Did you finish the blue series?

We talk, but not in the same language we used to. The cadence is off. The intimacy is thinner. We are trading updates, not souls. Her messages slow a little. Mine slow more. Communication becomes like low tide—still present, but receding, revealing the rocky distance between us.

IV. The Study Group & Sarah

Sarah Mitchell

I don't plan to join a group. I work better alone. But word travels that "Gray is the one to beat," and before long, students are asking if I want in on a rotating study schedule. I attend one session out of politeness, thinking it'll be a brief detour.

That's where I meet Sarah Mitchell again. We'd spoken briefly once before, at an undergrad mixer, but she wasn't someone I paid attention to beyond casual recognition. This time, she commands attention.

She is sitting at the head of the long library table. Sharp eyes behind wire-rimmed glasses, immaculate posture, blonde hair pulled back with surgical precision. She looks like she stepped out of a legal drama—but the kind where she wins every case and destroys the opposition.

"You're Gray," she says when I walk in. She doesn't stand up. "And you're Mitchell." Her smile tilts—sharp, amused. "Good. We remember each other. Have a seat. We're dissecting Palsgraf."

We sit across from one another. She reads at an alarming pace, flipping pages with the focus of someone dissecting the human genome. After half an hour, she leans back, capping her highlighter. "You're fast," she observes. "Fast in the way that means you'll be dangerous later." "Dangerous?" "In court. In negotiations. In anything that requires strategy. Most people here read to understand. You read to dismantle." "You say that like it's a warning." Her smile deepens. "It is."

And something inside me shifts—curiosity, maybe. Apprehension. Recognition of someone whose ambition mirrors mine but whose path was paved with fewer doubts. Sarah challenges me. She pushes me. She argues with me not to win, but to make the argument better. Everything with her feels... easier. Less emotional. Less risky. There is no ocean between us. There is only the table. And that ease is a danger all its own.

V. The Accelerant

The Dean's Offer

Two days before winter break of my first year, I'm summoned by Dean Holloway. His office is warm, filled with leather-bound books and awards that catch the light. Holloway looks at me like a scientist observing a particularly successful chemical reaction.

"Gray," he says, steepling his fingers. "You are performing beyond the expectations of this curriculum." "Thank you, sir." "That isn't a compliment. It's a logistical problem." "A... problem?" "You're learning too quickly. You're bored in Torts. I can see it. You're answering questions Lang hasn't even asked yet."

He pushes a document toward me across the mahogany desk. "This is a petition to complete your J.D. in two years. An accelerated track. Heavily loaded summers. Clinics concurrent with coursework."

I stare at the paper. It feels heavier than anything I've held this semester. Holloway leans forward. "Few students in this institution's history have earned this option. Your father did it." Of course he did.

"And the drawbacks?" I ask. "You'll be younger. Thrust into the field early. There will be resentment from your peers. Pressure. The burnout rate is high. But you can handle that."

I leave his office with the petition in hand and a hollowness in my chest I can't name. When I tell my father over dinner, he beams. He orders a bottle of expensive wine. When I tell my mother, she hides her fear behind pride, touching my cheek with a hand that trembles slightly. When I tell Jennie, she texts: You're remarkable. Truly. Just... don't forget to breathe.

The message feels sad in a way I don't know how to address. She is proud of me, but she is watching me speed up, moving faster and faster away from the boy who sat still on a cliff in Gangneung. I sign the petition anyway. Brilliance becomes a path. A destiny. A price.

VI. The Reunion

Echoes of Haesindang

The semester accelerates. I am taking eighteen credits. I sleep four hours a night. But one Friday in April, an unexpected text breaks the cycle. Lorenzo: We're in town. Beer? Or do you only drink the blood of your enemies now?

I meet them at a pub in Cambridge. Lorenzo, Michael, and Damion. They look exactly the same—loud, easy, comfortable in their own skin. We order a pitcher. We catch up. Then, inevitably, the conversation turns to Korea.

"Man, I still dream about that BBQ place in Mapo," Michael says, wiping foam from his lip. "And the DMZ," Damion adds. "That was heavy." "But nothing," Lorenzo grins, slamming his glass down, "beats the Penis Park."

A few law students at the next table turn their heads. They are wearing Patagonia vests and looking skeptical. "Excuse me?" one of them asks, amused. "Did you say Penis Park?"

"Haesindang Park," Lorenzo corrects, delighted to have an audience. "South Korea. A whole park. Dedicated to phalluses. Big ones. Small ones. Ones shaped like benches." The law students laugh. It is a cynical, elite laugh. "That sounds ridiculous," one girl says. "Why would anyone build that?"

I feel a spike of defensive heat in my chest. I think of Jennie. I think of the way she looked at the statues. I think of the lesson she taught me about reverence.

"It's not ridiculous," I say. My voice is quiet, but it carries the weight of the courtroom voice I am developing. The table goes quiet. "It's folklore," I continue, turning to the law students. "It's based on a legend of a virgin who drowned at sea. The fishermen couldn't catch anything afterward—they believed her spirit was angry. One day, a fisherman relieved himself into the ocean, and he caught fish. So they deduced that… the male energy appeased her."

The students are listening now. "It's tragic," I say. "And it's human. It's about a community trying to make sense of grief and starvation. They used humor and sexuality to bargain with death. It's actually… quite beautiful. In a raw way."

Silence. Then the girl nods slowly. "That's… actually fascinating." "It is," I say.

Lorenzo claps me on the shoulder. "See? That's why we bring the Professor. He makes dick jokes sound like poetry." Everyone laughs. But I don't laugh. I take a drink. The defense of the park felt good. But it also brought back the memory of Jennie so vividly it hurts. It reminds me of the gulf that currently exists between the man who defended the park and the man who is buried in case law. I check my phone under the table. No messages.

VII. The Almost

Sarah

Spring in Cambridge means thawing sidewalks and blooming magnolias and law students clutching outlines like lifelines. I move through my second year—which is really my final year—with an intensity that unnerves everyone around me. Even Lang comments once: "You work like someone running out of time, Gray." "I'm not." He raises an eyebrow. "Then what are you running from?" I don't answer.

Sarah becomes a fixture. We study together. Eat together sometimes. Debate relentlessly. She never crosses the line. She never pushes. But she watches me carefully.

One night, two weeks before finals, we are the last two people in the library. It is raining. The windows are dark mirrors reflecting our exhausted faces. We are debating a constitutional law case. We are standing close to the whiteboard, arguing about the Commerce Clause. She makes a point. I counter it. She laughs—a rare, genuine sound. "God, you're stubborn," she says. "I'm right." "You're usually both."

She steps closer. The air between us changes. It shifts from intellectual to physical. It is the static electricity of two people who understand each other perfectly. She looks up at me. Her eyes search mine. "Are you still with her?" she asks softly. "The girl in Korea?"

The question feels like an arrow. I look at Sarah. She is here. She is real. She understands the "suit." She understands the pressure. Loving her would be easy. It would make sense. It would be a merger of equals. "I don't know," I say honestly.

Sarah inhales. She leans in. Her hand brushes my arm. "You deserve someone who matches your world," she whispers. "Someone who understands this pace. Someone who doesn't ask you to slow down." I look at her lips. It would be so easy. "But maybe," she adds, pulling back just an inch, "you deserve someone who doesn't. Maybe you need the friction."

The moment hangs there, suspended. We don't kiss. But we both feel the shift. The door is unlocked.

VIII. The Break You Don't See Coming

Silence

That night, shaken by the near-miss with Sarah, I send Jennie a long message. I'm thinking about you today. About the cliffs. About Bonchon in Gangneung. About how your laugh sounds in the cold. I miss it. I miss us. I miss you. Please tell me we're still us.

She doesn't reply. Not that night. Not the next morning. Not the next week.

Silence settles between us like winter snow. Soft. Cold. Inescapable. I check my phone obsessively at first. Then less. Then occasionally. At some point, in the haze of finals prep, I stop checking at all.

Because the truth is simple: Something broke. Quietly. Slowly. Inevitably. There was no explosion. No fight. Just the slow erosion of distance and the relentless forward motion of my life in Boston. The "suit" grew too tight to fit the memory of the boy in Seoul.

IX. Graduation

Alone in a Crowd

Graduation is a blur of pomp and circumstance. The ceremony is held outdoors. The sky is a brilliant, mocking blue. Speeches about justice and leadership. Applause that sounds like rain. Shaking hands that feel foreign. My father claps me on the back, his face flushed with triumph. "Two years," he says to anyone who will listen. "Top of the class. A Gray tradition." My mother hugs me too tightly, smelling of expensive perfume and anxiety. Dean Holloway praises my accelerated completion. Professor Lang gives me a rare nod of respect as I walk off the stage.

Everyone sees me. Everyone celebrates me. Sarah finds me in the crowd. She looks stunning in her robes. She smiles, a knowing, sharp smile. "You made it," she says. "We made it."

But as I stand there, holding the diploma that certifies I am now officially what I was always meant to be, I check my phone one last time. Nothing. No message. No missed call. No "I'm proud of you."

I look up at the sky. I realized then that I have achieved everything I set out to do. I have secured the legacy. I have worn the suit. And I am entirely, completely alone in the crowd.

Chapter Fourteen: The Quiet Between Us

Edward

Boston in January is less a city and more a lesson in endurance.

It has a way of swallowing sound. The heavy, wet snow muffles the honking of taxis on Congress Street, the chatter of pedestrians, and even the hum of the subway that runs beneath the asphalt like a restless, metal vein. But the silence isn't peaceful. It isn't the contemplative, expansive silence of the mountains in Seoraksan, where the quiet felt like a presence. Here, the silence is expectant. It is the hush of a courtroom before a verdict is read.

I walk to the firm each morning with my breath fogging in front of me, a temporary ghost in the gray air. My scarf is tucked tightly against the cold—cashmere, a gift from my mother, soft but insufficient against the wind coming off the harbor.

My father arrives earlier than I do. He always has. It is his way of claiming the day before anyone else has a chance to touch it. But lately, the dynamic has shifted. He no longer looks at me like a subordinate he is forced to train. He looks at me like an investment that is finally beginning to mature. He looks at me like he is standing beside his successor, rather than dragging him from behind.

"You're settling in," he says one Tuesday morning.

I am sliding into my new office—a space that is technically an upgrade from the cubicle I occupied during my summer associate days, though it feels smaller. It has mahogany wainscoting and a view of a brick wall, but it has more bookshelves than I will ever fill.

I place my briefcase on the desk, aligning it with the edge. "Trying to," I say.

My father lingers in the doorway. He is wearing a suit that cost more than my first car, and he wears it with the casual indifference of a man who has never worried about the price of anything.

"The Anderson merger files are on your desk," he says. "I need a risk assessment on the environmental liabilities by tomorrow morning."

"I thought Miller was handling Anderson."

"Miller misses things. You don't." He pauses, his eyes scanning my desk, my coat, my face. "You're doing good work, Edward. The partners are noticing."

"Thank you."

"Don't get comfortable," he replies, tapping his knuckles against the doorframe. "Comfort makes you slow. Try harder."

Then he walks away, his footsteps sharp and rhythmic on the hardwood. That is his version of affection. He doesn't offer praise; he offers more weight to carry.

I sit down and stare at the stack of case files waiting for me. Family disputes buried in legalese. Contract reviews for tech startups. Arbitration prep for construction companies. I open the first file, and my mind slips into its familiar mode of analysis—dissecting facts, spotting contradictions, building arguments. It is a cold, mechanical comfort.

And yet, beneath the efficiency, something else pulses. A low ache. A quiet beat that refuses to synchronize with the ticking clock on the wall.

Where is Jennie? What time is it in Seoul? Did she finish the painting with the blue skyline? When did we stop being us?

The truth is, graduation didn't shatter us. The flight home didn't break us. Silence did. Distance did. Time zones that turned day into night did. Fear did. I did.

But admitting that is harder than any exam Lang ever threw at me. It requires a kind of honesty that doesn't bill by the hour.

The Exhibition Photo

Around noon, just as I am debating whether to eat a stale bagel or skip lunch entirely, my phone buzzes against the polished wood of my desk.

It's a message from Jennie.

For a moment, everything inside me freezes. My heart stutters the way it used to when her face would fill my screen in Seoul—warm, bright, smiling as if she carried sunlight in her pockets. The reaction is visceral, a physical rejection of the cold room I am sitting in.

I unlock the screen. She hasn't sent text. She's sent a photo.

It's from her gallery opening. She's standing in front of a large piece—a striking, shadowed photograph of a coastline I recognize instantly. The cliff at Haesindang. The one where the wind whipped her hair across her face and she laughed when I tried to imitate the tour guide's overly dramatic gestures. The one where we stood shoulder to shoulder, looking out at the water like we were peering into a future we never dared to say aloud.

In the photo, she looks older than I remember. Not aged, but… settled. She is wearing a deep green dress that leaves her shoulders bare, the color contrasting with her dark hair. Her hands are clasped in front of her. Her smile is small, polite, directed at the camera but not for the camera.

Something inside me twists sharply, a physical pain behind my ribs. She looks beautiful. And she looks entirely out of my reach.

I stare at the image, zooming in on her face, trying to find a trace of the girl who ate tteokbokki with me on a plastic stool in the rain. She is there, but she is hidden behind the artist, behind the success, behind the thousands of miles of ocean between us.

My thumb hovers over the keyboard. I type: You look incredible. I wish I was there. I stare at it. It feels too desperate. Too intimate for the silence that has grown between us over the last few weeks. Delete.

I type: Is that Haesindang? I remember that day. Too nostalgic. It sounds like I'm clinging to the past because I have nothing to offer in the present. Delete.

I type: I miss you. The cursor blinks at me. The truth sits there, three simple words that could change everything or change nothing. But fear—the fear of her pity, the fear of her silence—grips my hand.

Instead, I write: The exhibition looks impressive. Congratulations.

I press send before I can hate myself for it. It feels stiff. Distant. Cowardly. It sounds like something a colleague would send. It sounds like something my father would send.

I wait. The phone sits on the desk like a live grenade. Three minutes. Five minutes. Ten.

Finally, the screen lights up. Thank you.

Two words. Formal. Polite. Final.

That small message—that tiny, quiet message—lands harder than if she'd screamed at me. If she were angry, there would still be passion. If she were hurt, there would still be a connection. But politeness? Politeness is the funeral of intimacy.

I sit there for a long time after, staring at the message thread. It used to be filled with paragraphs, with inside jokes, with emojis, with late-night confessions about our fears and dreams. Now it's a skeleton. A ghost. A digital record of the slow, suffocating death of something we never learned to protect.

The Firm

My father expects excellence. But the firm expects ownership.

The culture at Gray, Miller & Associates is one of polite brutality. You are expected to be the first one in and the last one out. You are expected to treat every case, no matter how minor, as if it were a Supreme Court hearing.

He passes my office throughout the day, stopping occasionally to ask questions. "Did you find the precedent on the liability clause?" "Yes." "Did you cross-reference it with the 2018 ruling?" "Yes." "Good. Do it again."

I read faster. I work later. I take on more cases than any associate my age should. Not because I need to prove myself to him—I stopped needing his validation somewhere between my second and third year of law school—but because I don't want to stop.

If I stop, I have to think. If I think, I feel the ache. The ache that says: You lost her. And you did it slowly. Carelessly. Thoughtlessly.

One night, a Tuesday that feels like a Friday, I am still at my desk at 9:30 p.m., combing through the minutiae of a custody dispute involving assets in three different countries. My eyes burn. The coffee in my mug has gone cold hours ago.

"You're here late, Gray," a voice says from the doorway.

I look up, blinking against the harsh fluorescent light. Sarah.

She is leaning against the doorframe, holding a takeout container. Her silhouette is framed by the hallway light. She's wearing a dark wool coat, her hair pulled back in a severe, elegant bun. She has the same confidence she had at Harvard, but there is more polish now—an edge sharpened by clerking for a federal judge in D.C. for the past year.

"What brings you here?" I ask, rubbing my temples. "I thought you were climbing the ladder in Washington."

"I was meeting with one of the partners," she says, stepping into the room. She moves with a fluid, easy grace that belongs in these halls. "I'm rotating through firms this month. Interviewing. Seeing what fits."

"Does this one fit?"

She looks around the room, her gaze critical but not unkind. She takes in the towers of case files, the framed certificates, the stiff-backed chairs, the unspoken expectations hanging in the air like humidity.

"It depends what you want," she says, placing the takeout container on a stack of books. "Pad Thai. I ordered too much."

"I'm not hungry."

"You look starving," she counters. "Eat."

I open the container. The smell of peanuts and lime fills the sterile room, reminding me that I haven't eaten since breakfast. I take a plastic fork and take a bite. It's good.

Sarah sits in the client chair opposite me, crossing her legs. She watches me eat for a moment. "So," she says. "How is life under the Emperor?"

I smirk. "My father is… consistent."

"That's a polite way of saying 'tyrannical.'" She picks up a file, glances at the cover, and puts it down. "You're working on the Henderson divorce? That's grunt work, Edward. You're better than that."

"It needs to be done."

"By a junior associate. Not by the heir apparent." She leans forward, her elbows on her knees. Her eyes, intelligent and piercing, lock onto mine. "Why are you burying yourself, Edward?"

I chew slowly. "I'm working, Sarah. That's what we do."

"No," she says softly. "This is different. In law school, you worked because you were hungry. You wanted to win. Now? You look like you're working because you're trying to avoid going home."

I stop eating. The silence stretches between us. "I go home," I say defensively.

"To what?" I don't answer. She nods, as if I've confirmed a theory. "That's what I thought."

She stands up and walks to the window, looking out at the snow-dusted skyline of Boston. "You're different," she says quietly. "Since you came back from that trip. Since graduation."

"Different how?"

"Sharper," she says, tracing a finger along the windowsill. "Colder. More tired." She turns to face me. "And lonely."

I tense. My grip on the plastic fork tightens. "I'm fine, Sarah."

"Everyone says that right before they break," she replies. Her voice isn't mocking; it's gentle. It cuts deeper than mockery would.

She walks back to the desk. She doesn't push further. She never does. Her skill isn't force; it's presence. She has an uncanny ability to stand next to the truth until you are forced to look at it too.

"Have you talked to her?" she asks. She doesn't need to say the name. "We message," I say. "Messages aren't talking." "She's busy. I'm busy." "Bullshit," Sarah says. "People make time for what they want. If you aren't making time, and she isn't making time, then you're letting it die. Is that what you want?"

"No," I whisper. "Then fix it," she says. "Or let it go. But this—" she gestures to the piles of paperwork, the cold coffee, the dark circles under my eyes "—this purgatory you've built for yourself? It's going to kill you."

She buttons her coat. "Take care of yourself, Edward. No one else here will do it for you."

Then she leaves. Her footsteps echo down the hallway, fading into silence. A silence that feels too much like the one Jennie left behind. A silence that is filling up the room, displacing the air, making it hard to breathe.

Jennie

The days after the exhibition feel strangely anticlimactic.

Success, I am learning, doesn't taste like I thought it would. I expected champagne. I expected electricity. I expected the world to look brighter, saturated with color. Instead, it's quiet. Soft. Almost melancholy, as if the culmination of a dream only underscores the absence of the person I wanted to share it with.

Seoul moves on. The traffic on the Han River Bridge never stops. The neon lights of Hongdae flicker and buzz. I am standing in the center of it, successful, and I have never felt more invisible.

Sohee senses it immediately. Two nights after the opening, she drags me out of the studio. "You are not spending another night staring at a blank canvas," she announces, throwing my coat at me. "We are going out. Alcohol. Music. Bad decisions. Let's go."

We end up at a small, noisy pojangmacha tent in Mapo-gu. The plastic walls flap in the winter wind, but inside it is warm, smelling of spicy broth and grilled mackerel. The noise is deafening— shouting businessmen, clinking soju glasses, the hiss of the gas burner.

Sohee pours me a shot of soju. "Drink," she commands. I drink. It burns, a clean, sharp heat. "You're too young and too hot to be this sad," Sohee says, chewing on a piece of radish. "You look like a Victorian widow."

"I'm not sad," I lie, reaching for the fish cakes. "You're sad," she counters. "You're 'Artist-Sad.' It's worse. It's pretentious sadness." I roll my eyes. "What does that even mean?" "It means you feel things too much and turn them into tortured masterpieces instead of just crying and getting over it."

I throw a crumpled napkin at her. She ducks, laughing, her bright earrings catching the light. But then the laughter fades. She looks at me over the rim of her glass, her expression sobering.

"Have you heard from him?" she asks softly. The noise of the tent seems to drop away. "Not really," I say, staring at the swirling clear liquid in my glass. "Did he congratulate you at least? On the exhibition?" "Yes." "And?" "And nothing," I whisper. "He said congratulations. I said thank you."

Sohee slams her glass down on the plastic table. "That's it? 'Congratulations'? Like you just passed a driving test?" "He's busy, Sohee. He's a lawyer in a top firm. His father is—" "I don't care if his father is the Pope," she interrupts. "If a man loves you, he doesn't send a one-word text. He calls. He sends flowers. He flies here."

"It's complicated."

"It's not," she says, leaning forward. "It hurts. That's the only thing that matters. It hurts you. I see it."

I look down. The steam from the fish cake soup rises between us. "It hurts in a slow way," I admit, my voice barely audible. "Like a tide pulling at the shore, taking one grain of sand at a time. You don't notice it's happening until you look down and the ground is gone."

Sohee reaches across the table and squeezes my hand. Her grip is fierce. "So what are you going to do?" "I don't know."

I scroll through my phone later that night, lying in bed while the city glows orange outside my window. I could message him. I could send a voice note. I could call him right now. It's morning in Boston. He would be awake.

But I don't. Not because I don't want to. God, I want to. I want to hear his voice so badly my chest aches with it. But because I don't know what I am to him anymore.

Am I a memory? A pleasant semester abroad? Am I a complication? A distraction from his important cases and his demanding father? Am I a wound he is trying to heal? Or am I just something he loved once, but no longer knows how to hold?

I curl into my blankets and turn off the screen. I tell myself that distance isn't always abandonment. Sometimes it's just fear wearing a different name.

Edward

I don't know when the insomnia starts. Probably sometime after Jennie stops replying regularly. Probably sometime after Sarah looked at me with that pitying, knowing gaze. Probably sometime after my father handed me three new clients in one week and told me to "sink or swim."

Regardless, it's here now. A permanent resident in my apartment. Nights stretch long and empty. The hum of the refrigerator is deafening. The headlights sweeping across my ceiling are taunting.

I sit at my desk in my apartment, bathed in the blue light of my laptop. I am staring at case law regarding intellectual property theft. The words blur and sharpen in waves. Precedent. Liability. Damages. Intent.

I write emails I don't send. I draft texts to Jennie that I never finish. I hate it here. Come visit me. I think I'm forgetting what your voice sounds like.

Hours pass. 2:00 a.m. 3:00 a.m.

I check my phone. Nothing. I check again. Still nothing. The silence grows heavier than any workload I carry. It is a physical weight, pressing down on my lungs.

One night, as I force myself through deposition summaries, my father's voice floats up from my memory, unbidden. "Love is a distraction for men who haven't found their purpose yet. You build the castle first, Edward. Then you find someone to live in it."

And then my mother's voice, softer, from a time before she faded into the background of his life: "Love is not an inconvenience, Edward. It's a privilege. It's the only thing that makes the noise bearable. Don't forget that."

I don't know which one is right. Or if either is. What I do know is this: The more I rise professionally—the more partners nod at me in the hallway, the more my billable hours increase, the more my father pats my shoulder—the more I fall personally.

I am hollowing out. And ambition, once exhilarating, now feels like it's costing me something I can't replace.

A Call from an Old Ghost

I'm in the middle of drafting a motion to dismiss when my phone buzzes. I expect it to be a client. Or my father. Or perhaps Sarah, asking if I've eaten.

It's Jennie.

My breath catches. The world narrows down to the device in my hand. The message is short: How are you?

Nothing else. No photo. No "I miss you." Just a generic inquiry. The kind you send to an old classmate you haven't seen in five years.

I stare at the blinking cursor. I type: Busy. Exhausted. Miserable without you. Delete. I'm okay. Thinking of you constantly. Delete. I miss you. Please call me. Delete.

My fingers hover. I am a lawyer. I make a living with words. I can argue complex theories of negligence. I can persuade juries. But I cannot talk to the woman I love.

I type: I'm good.

Send.

Immediately, regret burns across my chest like acid. Good? I'm not good. I'm drowning. Why did I say I'm good? I wait. I pray for her to see through it. I pray for her to push back, to ask, Really? Because you don't seem good.

A minute passes. Five minutes. Twenty.

Her reply comes: Good. Just checking in.

Checking in. Like I'm an appointment. Like I'm someone she worries about vaguely, from a distance. Not someone she is connected to.

I stare at the phone until the screen dims to black. For the first time, the distance feels final. It feels like the ocean has finally swallowed us both.

The Night It Becomes Real

Two weeks later, the snow begins falling again. It is a soft, steady snowfall, drifting across the city like confetti at a celebration no one asked for. It covers the grit of the streets, turning Boston into something deceptively pure.

I stay late at the office. Everyone else leaves. The paralegals, the secretaries, the junior associates. Even my father leaves at 8:00 p.m., heading to a fundraising dinner.

At midnight, I step out of the building. The cold air hits me, sharp and biting. I wrap my scarf tighter. I start walking. I don't hail a cab. I just walk.

Boston is quiet. The streets are washed in pale orange streetlights. Snow gathers in delicate piles on the sidewalks, crunching under my dress shoes. I walk past the Common, past the frozen pond where ducks are huddled together for warmth. I walk past the stately brick buildings of Beacon Hill that house so many dreams and so many fractured ambitions.

I feel entirely alone. And for the first time, I wonder if this is it. If this is the rest of my life. Walking alone in the cold, successful and empty.

My phone buzzes in my pocket. It vibrates against my hip, a jarring intrusion. I stop walking. I stand under a streetlamp, the snow falling around me in a cone of light.

I pull it out. Not Jennie. Not Sarah. Not my parents.

It's a news alert. **BREAKING: Rumors swirl regarding investigation into Governor John F. Lincoln's campaign finances.**

I frown. Some vague public rumor about improper donations. Speculation. Nothing confirmed. Nothing yet. But the timing feels ominous. The wording is specific. Whistleblower. Ethics committee.

It feels like the first tremor of an earthquake. Like something large is shifting in the shadows, waiting to devour everything in its path.

I close the notification. I shove the phone back into my pocket, deep, trying to hide it from the cold. I don't know it yet, but this night—this quiet, cold, lonely night—is the end of one life and the beginning of another.

The life where I still had hope of repairing something with Jennie is ending. The life where I still had room to breathe is closing. The life where my father's ambitions hadn't swallowed mine whole is gone.

The storm is coming. And I'm not ready.

Jennie

The snow reaches Seoul too. It is different snow. Wet. Heavy. Mixing with the pollution to turn gray before it hits the ground. Different sky. Different ache.

I stand in the doorway of my studio, watching flakes drift past the neon haze of a 24-hour convenience store across the street.

The gallery called today—they want more pieces. They want a series. My residency mentor wants me to apply for a fellowship in Jeju Island. Sohee wants me to go out and meet someone new. An architect, she said. "He likes art. He has nice hands."

Everyone wants something for me. Except the one person I used to want something with.

I open my phone. I scroll through old messages. I stop on the last one.

I'm good.

It hurts. It sits there on the screen, a lie we both agreed to tell. But I breathe through it. Maybe love isn't always meant to last forever. Maybe the person we loved at twenty isn't the person we're meant to love at twenty-three. Maybe distance is a teacher disguised as a thief, taking away what we don't need so we can find what we do.

Or maybe— As I stare out into the snowy street, watching a couple walk by under a shared umbrella, holding each other tight against the wind— Maybe some stories aren't over. Not really.

Maybe they're just waiting for the world to break so they can be put back together.

I turn off the lights. I lock the door. I walk out into the snow, alone, but walking forward. Waiting. Just waiting for it.

Chapter Fifteen: The Ascent and the Cost

Edward

The call from my father comes at 11:37 p.m., sharp enough to cut through the exhaustion fogging my brain. I am staring at a contract for a merger I don't care about, the words swimming like oil on water.

"Edward," he says without preamble. His voice is clipped, urgent in a way I've rarely heard. My father is a man of tectonic slowness; he moves only when the earth requires it. This is different. "You need to get down here. Now."

I stand from my desk instinctively, my spine cracking from hours of stasis. "What's happened?"

"It's Governor Lincoln."

A pause — the kind of pause heavy enough to rearrange a life.

"He's requesting you. Personally."

A strange stillness settles over me, silencing the hum of the HVAC system and the distant sirens of Boston.

Governor John F. Lincoln. The political golden boy. The man who shook my hand once at a cocktail mixer two years ago, held my gaze a second too long, and looked at me like he was cataloging potential. Like he was shopping for a weapon. The candidate many quietly whispered might one day run for President.

And he wants… me?

"I'll be there," I say.

I hang up, grab my coat, and step out into the icy Boston night. The wind off the harbor tastes of salt and diesel. It is a cold, hard scent— nothing like the humid, street-food sweetness of a Seoul evening. I push that thought away. I have become very good at pushing thoughts of her away.

I. Arrival

The firm is lit up like daylight when I arrive. It's midnight, but the building is vibrating with a frantic, terrified energy. Senior associates rush through corridors, faces tight, voices low, eyes darting to screens filled with headlines and leaked allegations. The air smells of burnt coffee and fear.

My father meets me outside his office. He looks older tonight. The lines around his mouth are etched deep, filled with the shadows of a crisis he can't control.

"How bad is it?" I ask, stripping off my coat.

He exhales, a sound like a tire losing air. "Worse than bad."

He hands me a tablet. The screen glows blue in the dim hallway, illuminating the headline in bold:

GOVERNOR JOHN F. LINCOLN UNDER INVESTIGATION FOR ETHICS VIOLATIONS Anonymous whistleblower alleges improper procurement dealings and pay-to-play schemes.

My stomach tightens. In this city, an accusation is a verdict. The truth is merely an appeal filed too late.

"What's real?" I ask, scrolling through the article. It's vague, damaging, designed to bleed him out slowly.

"No one knows yet. That's why he wants you."

Me. Not the senior partners with their thirty years of experience and their names on the door. Not the crisis management team with their spin doctors and media connections. Me. The associate. The grinder. The one who doesn't sleep.

My father studies me, his eyes narrowing. He sees something in me, I think. He sees the change that has happened since I came back from Korea. He sees the hollowness that makes me efficient.

"He remembers you from Holloway's event," my father says. "And from the Lang deposition. He said he wants the 'kid who dissected the witness like a frog.'"

My pulse quickens—a spike of adrenaline, sharp and addictive. I take the tablet back. "Where is he?"

"In the conference room. With the wolves."

I push open the heavy glass doors. The room is thick with tension. A half-dozen senior partners are sitting around the periphery, looking useless. Governor John F. Lincoln stands at the head of the table, sleeves rolled up, tie loosened. His face looks carved from exhaustion — sharp, severe, but still charismatic in a way born from decades of public life. He has the kind of presence that changes the air pressure in a room.

He turns when I enter. His eyes are blue steel, unblinking.

"Gray," he says, with a small, humorless smile. "Good. Let's begin."

There's no greeting. No handshake. No warming up. Just crisis.

II. The Files

Lincoln slides a thick stack of folders across the polished mahogany table. The sound of the paper sliding is the only sound in the room.

"Everything," he says. "At least, everything we know. My staff is currently scrubbing the servers to preserve data, but this is the raw feed."

I pull a chair out and sit. The other partners are watching me. I can feel their resentment radiating like heat. Why him? they are thinking. Why the boy?

I open the first file. It hits like a tidal wave:

Misallocation of public funds regarding the grandiose construction projects in Springfield.

Conflicting donor disclosures buried in shell corporations.

Inconsistencies in procurement records for state technology contracts.

A whistleblower claiming private influence from a foreign lobby.

Emails that don't align with timestamps.

Travel logs that don't match receipts.

A suspiciously clean sequence of anonymous leaks dropped to the Globe and the Times simultaneously.

This isn't just a scandal. It's an assassination. A career-ending storm engineered to leave nothing standing.

Lincoln sits opposite me, elbows on the table, fingers pressed to his temple. He looks smaller than he does on television, but denser. Like a dying star.

"I didn't do this," he says quietly.

I look up. Most clients lie. They lie to their wives, they lie to the police, and they lie to their lawyers. Especially the politicians. But something in his tone — not defensive, not manipulative, just tired — makes me pause.

"I want to see everything," I say. "Not just the files. I want your personal calendar. I want your texts. I want the GPS data from your security detail's SUVs."

A senior partner, Miller, scoffs from the corner. "Edward, that's excessive. We need to focus on the legal precedents for—"

Lincoln holds up a hand, silencing Miller without even looking at him. He keeps his eyes on me.

"Give him what he wants," Lincoln commands the room. Then to me: "Read. And tell me how I survive."

The way he says it — not if he survives, but how — sends a chill through me. It is a command to alter reality.

I gather the folders. I ignore the glares of the senior partners. I ignore the shaking of my father's head. I start reading.

Page after page. Hour after hour. The room empties out. The partners leave to go home to their families. The Governor retreats to a side office to make calls. It is just me. And the puzzle. And the silence.

In the silence, usually, thoughts of Jennie come. The way she laughed covering her mouth. The smell of rain on the pavement in Seoul. The warmth of her hand. But tonight, the data is too loud. The numbers are screaming. I let the work drown her out. It is a relief to drown.

III. The First Breakthrough

By dawn, the city outside is gray and lifeless. My eyes burn like they've been rubbed with sand. My fingers ache from typing notes into my secure laptop.

But something surfaces. It's faint. A ghost in the machine. A pattern beneath the noise. A timeline that doesn't quite click.

"Governor," I say. My voice sounds raspy, unused for hours.

He appears in the doorway instantly, holding a cup of black coffee. He hasn't slept.

"Talk to me," he says.

"These emails—" I point to a sequence of leaked messages printed on glossy paper. They are damning. They supposedly show Lincoln authorizing a kickback to a construction firm. "The metadata is wrong."

He frowns, walking over. "Wrong how? My IT guys said they looked authentic."

"The time stamps claim you sent these at 11:06 p.m. from your home office on the 12th of November."

"Yes. I work late. You know that."

"Except your phone location—which I pulled from the raw data dump of your security detail—shows you at the Springfield fundraiser at that exact time. You were physically two hundred miles away from your home router."

He stares at the paper. "I could have sent it from my phone."

"You could have," I agree. "But the server log shows an IP address from a hardline connection. A desktop. Specifically, a desktop running an OS version that your office updated three months prior to this date."

I flip pages rapidly, adrenaline cutting through the exhaustion like a drug.

"And look at the syntax," I say, tapping the text. "You use the Oxford comma. Religiously. I checked your speeches, your memos, your personal letters. In these three incriminating emails? No Oxford comma. And the sign-off. You always write 'Best,' or 'Regards,'. This one says 'Thanks,'. You never say 'Thanks,'."

Lincoln leans forward, interest sparking in his tired eyes. He sees it now. The construct. The artifice.

"So?" he asks.

"So someone forged this chain," I say. "Or altered it. They copy-pasted your header onto a fabricated body."

A beat of silence. Then he exhales, a long, shuddering breath. "Show me more."

I walk him through it: the phrasing anomalies, the IP inconsistencies, the metadata inconsistencies across devices. I show him where the travel logs overlap with credit card receipts in impossible ways—buying gas in Boston twenty minutes after buying dinner in D.C.

By the end, Lincoln sits back in his chair, eyes sharper than when I arrived. The fear is gone, replaced by a cold, predatory focus.

"You found this in one night," he says.

I shrug. "It was there."

"No," he corrects. "It was buried. Deep."

He looks at me like he did at the dean's reception years ago. Like he's seeing the outline of someone dangerous. Someone useful.

"Keep going," he says. "Find the rest. Burn it all down."

IV. Becoming the Machine

For the next six months, I cease to be a person. I become an instrument.

My world shrinks to the four walls of the war room, the hum of the server, and the erratic orbit of Governor Lincoln.

The allegations keep coming, but now we are ready for them. Every time the press drops a bombshell, I am there to defuse it before it hits the ground.

The work consumes me in a way that's both terrifying and exhilarating. It is simpler than life. In the law, there are rules. Even the breaking of rules follows a logic. Human relationships—Jennie, my parents, my friends—have no logic. They are messy. They hurt. Here, in the data, nothing hurts.

I lose track of time. I lose track of meals. I eat vending machine crackers and drink lukewarm coffee. I lose track of daylight. I enter the building when it is dark and leave when it is dark. I lose track of who I was before this.

Associates whisper about me in the breakroom. They stop talking when I walk in. I am the twenty-six-year-old phenom who doesn't sleep, who sees patterns no one else can, who reads like a machine and reasons like a savant. They hate me. I don't care.

Sarah, a junior associate I used to grab lunch with, stops by my office twice. The first time, she brings a sandwich. "You look awful," she says gently. "Like a vampire." "I don't have time to look good. I have to depose the Chief of Staff in three hours." "Edward," she murmurs, "you can't keep going like this. You're going to snap."

But I don't snap. I harden. Because every night, as I connect more dots, uncover more anomalies, dismantle more accusations, I feel closer to something I don't have a name for. Power, maybe. Validation. Escape. All of them.

V. And Jennie...

The distance between us becomes a physical thing. A chasm widening with every hour I spend in that office.

When I first came back, we spoke every day. Then every week. Now, it is a sporadic ping in the darkness of my digital life.

Every once in a while, she messages me. Sometimes it's simple: Saw a painting today at the gallery in Insadong. Lots of blue. Thought of you.

Or: You must be tired. Take care of yourself, Edward.

Each message slices me open. It reminds me that there is a world where color exists, where people walk slowly and look at art. A world I voluntarily left.

Sometimes I reply quickly, typing with frantic thumbs in the elevator. Most times I reply late. Sometimes not at all.

Because every time I write her, the ache swells unbearably. To speak to her is to admit how miserable I am. To speak to her is to realize how cold Boston is.

During the height of Lincoln's investigation, on a Tuesday at 3:00 a.m., she sends: Are you okay? You seem so far away lately. I feel like I'm talking to a memory.

I stare at the screen. The cursor blinks. I type: I'm drowning. I hate this. I want to come back. Delete.

I miss you. I miss the food. I miss your voice. Delete.

I'm trying to build something here. Just wait for me. Delete.

I'm fine. Just busy. Send.

Her reply comes hours later. Okay. Let me know if you need anything.

And that — that polite, distant, beautiful line — hurts more than if she had screamed at me. Because she's giving up. She is retreating. She is learning to live without me, just as I am learning to live without myself. And I'm letting her.

VI. The Collapse

One night, around 2:50 a.m., the breakthrough turns into an avalanche.

I am cross-referencing the whistleblower's leaked testimony against the Governor's old EZ-Pass records. The whistleblower—a former disgruntled aid named Halloway—claims a meeting took place on April 14th at a private club in Worcester to discuss illegal zoning permits.

But Lincoln wasn't there. He wasn't even in that part of the state.

I pull up the footage from a local news archive. Lincoln is standing in a school auditorium in Danvers, addressing a room full of teachers. The timestamp on the news feed is verifiable. He is shaking hands, smiling, looking alive. I watch the footage twice. Then a third time. Then I check the metadata of the whistleblower's statement. It was filed two weeks ago, but the "notes" he claims to have taken were created digitally... yesterday.

I call him. He answers on the first ring. "Edward?" "Found something," I say. "The kill shot."

He arrives at the firm forty minutes later wearing sweatpants and a bomber jacket. His hair is rumpled, his eyes bloodshot. He looks more human than the polished politician on TV, and for a second, I see the man beneath the ambition. He is terrified of losing everything.

I show him the proof. I show him the doctored timestamp on Halloway's notes. I show him the video of the Danvers speech.

He watches the video, jaw tightening until a muscle feathers in his cheek. "Son of a bitch," he whispers. "Halloway lied. He fabricated the whole meeting."

"Governor," I say, leaning back, the tension finally leaving my shoulders. "This is the crack. If we pull at this, the entire case falls apart. If Halloway lied about the meeting, everything else is fruit of the poisonous tree. The credibility of the investigation evaporates."

Lincoln looks at me — really looks at me — and a strange emotion flickers across his face. It is gratitude, yes, but something else. Recognition. "Your father was right," he says softly. "You're a force of nature."

I don't respond. Because part of me is proud. The part of me that craves his approval, that craves the power he represents. And part of me is horrified by how much that pride matters. Part of me knows that to be a "force of nature" is to be something destructive.

VII. The Turning Point

With the timeline unraveling, the house of cards collapses. I lead the offensive. I am no longer defending; I am hunting.

One by one, I dismantle each accusation with surgical precision:

The Donor Money: I trace the "coordinations" to a rival campaign aide who planted the funds to look like a bribe.

The Procurement: I find the inconsistencies are actually clerical errors made by the state, not fraud by the Governor.

The Emails: We prove they were fabricated using an external server farm in Eastern Europe.

The Server Breach: I prove it was masked as routine maintenance by a contractor who had been paid off.

I draft the motions. I prep the Governor for the ethics committee. I write the opening statement for the senior partner to read, putting the words in his mouth because he doesn't understand the data like I do.

My father watches from the sidelines, equal parts awed and unnerved. He comes into my office one evening as I am shredding drafts. "You're surpassing me," he says. He tries to smile, but it doesn't reach his eyes. "And faster than I expected." "I'm just doing the job, Dad." "No," he says. "You're becoming the job. There's a difference." It should be a compliment. It sounds like a warning.

VIII. The Cataclysmic Victory

When the ethics committee finally clears Lincoln, the announcement is broadcast statewide. No fault. No violation. Total exoneration.

The firm erupts. Champagne corks pop. Secretaries are crying. Partners are slapping each other on the back, claiming credit for work they didn't do.

I stand in the back of the conference room, watching the television. Lincoln stands at the podium, cameras flashing, reporters leaning forward like hungry dogs. He looks invincible again. The exhaustion has been painted over with victory.

He doesn't mention my name — strategically. He can't admit that a twenty-six-year-old saved him; it makes him look weak. But when our eyes meet across the room through the screen—or maybe just in my mind—he nods once. A silent exchange: You saved me. Now we move.

Afterward, the party is in full swing at the firm. I am drinking scotch I don't like. Lincoln pulls me aside into a quiet hallway, away from the noise. "You did the impossible," he says. "You turned chaos into clarity. You saved my life, Edward." He straightens his jacket, eyes blazing with a terrifying, renewed fire. "Now I'm running."

I blink. "For re-election?" "No." He steps closer, lowering his voice. "The investigation made me a martyr. The exoneration makes me a hero. The timing is perfect. I'm running for President."

I stare at him. The country. The world stage. The White House. The beginning of something massive.

"What do you need from me?" I ask. I should say no. I should say I'm tired. I should say I need to go to Korea.

He smiles — sharp, confident, terrifying. "Everything. I want you as my Deputy Legal Counsel. I want you in D.C. next month."

My heart hammers. "Washington?" "Washington. That's where the real game is played. You've outgrown Boston, Edward. You've outgrown this firm."

IX. The Rise

It happens faster than I expect. Lincoln announces his exploratory committee three weeks later. Then his candidacy. Then his first round of endorsements. Then his polling surge.

Within months, he becomes the party's front-runner. The narrative of the "Unbroken Governor" is irresistible. And I become the voice he trusts most.

I move to D.C. I get an apartment I rarely see. Every morning at dawn, my phone rings: "What's today's risk profile, Edward?" Every night past midnight: "Walk me through tomorrow's opportunities." Every crisis: "Where is Gray? Get me Gray."

My father beams whenever I appear on internal campaign memos. He calls me to talk strategy, his voice filled with a respect he never showed me when I was a child. My mother is proud but frightened. "Edward," she says over dinner during a brief stopover in Boston. "You look… thinner." "I'm working, Mom." "You're disappearing," she whispers, touching my hand. Her hand feels paper-thin. I don't answer. She's not wrong. I am eroding. The wind of ambition is sanding me down to the bone.

X. The Broken Thread

Through all of this — the accolades, the rising political storm, the praise from Lincoln, the quiet envy from senior attorneys — there remains one constant ache. A phantom limb pain.

Jennie.

I haven't heard her voice in six months. The time difference makes it impossible. When I am awake, she is sleeping. When she is awake, I am in meetings that determine the future of the country.

One night, between depositions for a nuisance lawsuit against the campaign, I open our message thread. I scroll up. The last message from her reads: Be well, Edward.

Two words. No anger. No bitterness. Just a closing of a door I left cracked too long. It is the sound of resignation.

My chest tightens, a physical squeeze around my heart. I pour another drink of the cheap whiskey I keep in my desk drawer. I type: I'm sorry. Delete.

I miss you. God, I miss you. Delete.

Are you okay? Did you finish the painting? Delete.

I've been thinking about you. I'm coming back soon. Delete.

In the end, I write nothing. I turn off the phone. Silence sits there like a monument to everything I've failed to say. I am a successful lawyer. I am the right hand of the next President. I am a success. And I am entirely alone.

XI. The Moment Before Everything Changes

It's raining the night it happens — a soft, relentless drizzle against my apartment windows in D.C., the city glowing in the wet light. The Washington Monument is a faint needle in the distance, piercing the clouds.

I just finished a call with Lincoln. He was manic, excited about the Iowa poll numbers. He spoke with the certainty of a man who believes destiny is his employee. "Get some rest, Edward," he said. "We have a war to fight tomorrow."

I debated pushing through the electoral college briefing, but Governor Lincoln's voice echoed in my mind: we have a war to fight tomorrow. Generals always preach rest before battle, so I decided sleep was the better strategy at this juncture. Just before closing my laptop, I glanced at the mirror oddly positioned to my left. My reflection stared back. Pale. Dark circles. Eyes that looked older than twenty-seven. The price of success was staring at me—the eyes of a forty-year-old in a young man's body. Life was accelerating faster than I could handle. I needed to recharge just to reclaim my own age. I rubbed my eyes and breathed deeply. The air in the apartment finally felt conducive to rest—not too warm, not too cold, and for once, not stale. I was actually going to sleep early.

Chapter Sixteen: The Return

The message arrives at 11:42 p.m. on a Tuesday.

My phone vibrates against the mahogany desk. One short buzz.

I ignore it. I am trained to ignore it. In the last six months, my brain has been rewired to filter out anything that isn't a crisis, a poll number, or a direct order from Governor Lincoln. Plus, I just committed to getting more rest for the good of my body.

It buzzes again.

I sigh, rubbing the grit from my eyes, and flip the phone over. I expect it to be the Campaign Manager. Or perhaps my father, checking to see if I've reviewed the liability clauses.

It isn't. The name on the screen freezes the blood in my veins. I double checked the country code, and it is +82. My heart stumbles. My throat closes. The room suddenly feels very small. I reach out, my hand trembling slightly.

It has been months since we had a conversation that didn't feel like two satellites passing in the dark. My thumb hovers over the notification. I unlock the phone, my breath hitching in a way that has nothing to do with politics and everything to do with the Edward the young man that once found someone and then lose them.

The message is short.

Edward… I need to tell you something.

Nothing else. No explanation. No voice note. No emojis to soften the blow. Just a single sentence from a woman who once occupied my every thought, my every hope, my every wish whispered into the salt air over the East Sea.

I stare at the message for so long the screen dims and locks, forcing me to relive the moment by unlocking it again. I need to tell you something.

The phrasing is heavy. It carries the specific, suffocating weight of finality. It is not the casual checking-in of a lover; it is the prelude to an ending.

I call her immediately. The phone rings. One ring. (My heart hammers against my ribs.) Two rings. (I stand up, knocking my chair back.) Three rings. Then her voicemail picks up—her soft voice saying her name in Korean, then English, followed by a beep. I hang up. I call again. Straight to voicemail.

She has turned her phone off. She dropped the grenade and walked away.

Panic, cold and sharp, spikes in my chest. Why now? Why after so long? Why this tone?

My mind, trained to catastrophize by months of legal crisis management, begins to spin. Is she sick? Is she hurt? Has she found someone else? Or is it something worse—is she tired? Is she finally tired of waiting for a man who sends three-word texts between briefing papers?

I look at the laptop. The Lincoln campaign strategy. The future of the country. The career I killed myself to build. I look at the phone. The silence of the apartment screams at me.

I need to see her. Not eventually. Not when the campaign slows (it never slows). Not after the election. Now.

Before I can overthink it, before the lawyer in me can draft a list of reasons why this is professional suicide, I am moving. I grab my coat. I grab my passport from the safe. I grab my wallet. I leave the laptop open. I leave the lights on. I walk out into the rain-laced night, and for the first time in two years, I am not running toward an ambition. I am running toward a lifeline.

I. The Cost of Leaving

The firm's D.C. satellite office is still active when I stop by to grab my personal tablet. My father is there, unsurprisingly, reviewing litigation updates with two senior partners in a glass-walled conference room.

He sees me barrel through the hallway, drenched, hair plastered to my forehead, eyes wild. He excuses himself and steps out, closing the door behind him.

"Edward? What on earth—you look like you've seen a ghost."

"I need to take leave," I say. My voice sounds foreign to my own ears—raw, unpolished.

My father blinks, his composure rippling. "Leave? Now? We have the donor summit in three days. The Governor is counting on you to prep the ethics statement."

"I don't care about the ethics statement."

The silence that follows is absolute. My father stares at me as if I have started speaking a dead language. "Excuse me?"

"I'm taking a leave of absence. Effective immediately."

"For how long?"

"I don't know. A week. A month. Maybe forever."

He steps closer, his face tightening into the mask of the Managing Partner. "Son, listen to me. Governor Lincoln is preparing to announce his run for the Presidency. You are his most trusted legal advisor. You are on the shortlist for Deputy White House Counsel if he wins. Do you understand what you are throwing away?"

"I understand perfectly," I snap, the heat in my voice surprising us both. "I am throwing away a life I hate to save the only thing I actually love."

His jaw sets. "Is this about the girl? The painter?"

"Her name is Jennie."

"Edward, be rational. You haven't seen her in years. You are romanticizing a vacation fling because you are burnt out. Take a weekend. Go to the Hamptons. Sleep. But do not get on a plane to Korea."

I look at my father. I see the lines on his face, the gray in his hair, the hollowness in his eyes that no amount of success has ever filled. I see the future he wants for me—a mirror image of his own solitary, prestigious, empty existence.

"I'm not burnt out," I say, my voice dropping to a whisper. "I'm waking up."

"If you walk out that door," he warns, his voice low, "Lincoln will not take you back. I cannot protect you from the fallout."

126

I feel the weight of his words. I feel the terrifying vertigo of jumping off a cliff without a parachute. I think of Lincoln. I think of the power. I think of the history books. Then I think of Jennie's laugh. I think of the way she looks at the sea.

"I don't want you to protect me," I say. I turn my back on him. "I want you to understand me. But if you can't, I'm going anyway."

I walk to the elevator. I don't look back. The doors slide shut, severing the connection between the man I was supposed to be and the man I am becoming.

II. Time stands still

The flight to Seoul is fourteen hours of purgatory.

I managed to bribe my way onto the last seat of a Korean Air flight leaving Dulles—a middle seat in economy, wedged between a crying toddler and an elderly man snoring with the force of a chainsaw. I don't care. I would have strapped myself to the wing.

The cabin lights dim. The plane hums, a vibration that rattles in my bones. I close my eyes, but sleep is impossible. My mind replays the message. I need to tell you something.

What is it? The lawyer in me runs scenarios, analyzing the evidence. Hypothesis A: She met someone. This is the most likely statistical outcome. Long-distance relationships have a success rate of nearly zero. She is beautiful, talented, and kind. Why would she wait for a ghost who lives in a time zone twelve hours away? Hypothesis B: She is moving. Maybe to Europe. Maybe to the countryside. She wants to say goodbye before she disappears. Hypothesis C: She is sick. The thought makes my stomach lurch so violently I have to grip the armrests. No. Not that. Anything but that.

I pull out my phone, even though it's in airplane mode. I scroll through our history. The photos from the hike in Seoraksan. The video of us eating street food in Myeongdong, her face smeared with sauce, laughing as I try to wipe it off. The texts.

Edward: I miss you. Jennie: Look at the moon. I'm looking at it too.

Edward: Work is killing me. Jennie: Don't let it kill the best parts of you.

Edward: (No response for 3 days) Jennie: Be well, Edward.

I trace the glass screen with my thumb. I have been negligent. I have been arrogant. I thought she would wait forever. I thought I could pause her like a movie and come back when the intermission of my career was over. But life doesn't pause. Entropy applies to love just as it applies to the law. Things fall apart if you don't hold them together.

"Please," I whisper into the darkness of the cabin, a prayer to a God I haven't spoken to since law school. "Please let me be in time."

III. The Peninsula

I land in Incheon at 4:30 p.m. on a Wednesday. The air outside the terminal hits me like a physical blow—cold, dry, smelling of diesel and dust and roasted sweet potatoes. It smells like memory.

I hail a taxi. "Where to?" the driver asks in Korean. My Korean is rusty, degrading from lack of use. "Seoul," I say. "Mapo-gu. Her studio."

But as the taxi merges onto the highway, a notification pops up on my phone. A social media alert I set up years ago and forgot to disable. Jennie just checked in at Haesindang Park.

Haesindang. Samcheok. The coast. Three hours away.

It stops me cold. She went there. She went to the place of waiting.

"Change of plans," I tell the driver, leaning forward. "I need to go to Samcheok." The driver looks at me in the rearview mirror. "That's a long drive, sir. Very expensive." "I'll pay double," I say, handing him a wad of cash I exchanged at the airport. "Just drive."

The journey is a blur of tunnels and mountains. The city fades into the industrial outskirts, which fade into the rugged, snow-dusted peaks of Gangwon province. I watch the world pass. I feel like an astronaut re-entering the atmosphere—burning up, stripping away layers of protection, hurtling toward impact.

IV. The Cliffside

We arrive just as the sun is beginning its descent. The light is turning that specific, bruising purple that only exists in winter evenings. The wind at the coast is ferocious. It whips off the East Sea, carrying salt spray that stings the eyes.

I pay the driver and step out. The park is nearly empty. It's too cold for tourists. I walk up the winding path, past the wooden totem poles, past the pine trees bent by years of wind. My dress shoes slip on the gravel. I am underdressed in my D.C. wool coat, but I don't feel the cold. My adrenaline is a furnace.

I crest the hill that overlooks the ocean. And there she is.

She is sitting on the bench facing the water—the same bench where we once sat and talked until the stars came out. She is wrapped in a thick cream-colored coat, a red scarf wound multiple times around her neck. Her hands are deep in her pockets. She is staring at the horizon, where the gray sea meets the gray sky.

She looks small. She looks lonely.

I stop. The sound of my shoes on the gravel is lost to the roar of the waves. I just watch her for a second. The curve of her shoulder. The way her dark hair escapes her scarf and dances in the wind. I am afraid to speak. I am afraid to break the image.

"Jennie," I say. My voice is torn away by the wind, but she hears it. She stiffens. Her posture goes rigid. She turns slowly, as if she is afraid of what she will see.

When her eyes meet mine, the air leaves the world. Her eyes are wide, dark, and filled with a profound, shattering sadness. There is no smile. No rush of joy. Just a shock that looks painful.

"Edward?" she whispers.

I walk toward her. My legs feel heavy. "I got your message."

She stands up, clutching her coat tighter around herself. She looks at me as if I am a hallucination. "You... you're here." "I'm here." "But you're in Washington. You're working." "Not anymore."

She shakes her head, a small, jerky motion. She looks down at her boots, then back at me. Tears are beginning to pool in her eyes, but they aren't happy tears. They are the tears of someone who has been bracing for a collision.

"You shouldn't have come," she says, her voice trembling.

The words hit me like stones. "What?"

"You shouldn't have come, Edward." She steps back, putting distance between us. "I didn't ask you to come."

"You said you needed to tell me something."

"I could have said it over the phone. I wanted to say it over the phone because I knew… I knew if I saw you, I wouldn't be able to do it."

A cold dread settles in my stomach, heavier than the fear I felt on the plane. "Do what, Jennie? Tell me."

She looks out at the ocean, refusing to meet my gaze. The wind whips her hair across her face. "I wanted to tell you that I'm letting you go."

V. The Truth

The silence that follows is louder than the waves. I feel like I've been punched. "Let me go?" I repeat, the words tasting like ash. "What does that mean?"

She turns to me, and the anguish on her face breaks my heart. "It means I'm done, Edward. I'm done waiting. I'm done hoping."

"Jennie, I know I've been busy, I know I've been distant, but—"

"It's not just that!" she cries out, her voice cracking. "It's you. Look at you. You're soaring. I read the articles. I see the photos. You're standing next to the future President. You're building a kingdom."

"I'm building it for us," I plead.

"No," she says firmly, shaking her head. "You're building it for you. And that's okay. You should. You are brilliant and you are ambitious and you deserve the world. But I…" Her voice drops. "I am just a painter in Seoul. I am the thing that tethers you to the ground when you want to fly."

"That's not true."

"It is true. Every time we talk, I feel your guilt. I feel you rushing to get off the phone. I feel you torn in half." She takes a breath, shivering. "It hurts, Edward. It hurts to love you. It hurts to wake up every morning wondering if today is the day you finally forget me completely. I can't do it anymore. I don't have the strength."

She wipes a tear furiously from her cheek. "So I decided. I'm going to make it easy for you. I'm setting you free. Go be the great man you're supposed to be. Without the burden of me."

She looks at me with a tragic resolve. She thinks she is doing a noble thing. She is sacrificing her heart to save my career. She turns to walk away. To walk past me and down the path, out of my life forever.

VI. The Fight

Panic explodes in my chest—hot, white, blinding. If I let her walk past me, it's over. I know it. I will get back on a plane, I will become the White House Counsel, I will marry a senator's daughter I don't love, and I will spend the rest of my life bleeding internally.

I grab her arm. "No."

She flinches, stopping. "Edward, please. Don't make this harder."

"No," I say again, louder this time. I pull her around to face me. "You don't get to decide for me. You don't get to decide what my happiness looks like."

"I am trying to save you!" she yells, pushing at my chest.

"Save me from what?" I yell back, the raw emotion ripping through my lawyer's composure. "From loving you? From being human?"

"From regretting me!" she sobs. "Ten years from now, when you're not President because you had a distracted wife in Korea, you'll hate me. I won't let you hate me."

"I could never hate you." I step closer, invading her space, forcing her to look at me. The rain begins to fall, mixing with the sea spray, drenching us both.

"You think I'm soaring?" I ask, my voice shaking. "Jennie, I am miserable. I am drowning. I wake up every day in a city I hate, surrounded by people who would stab me in the back for a promotion, and the only thing, the only single thing that lets me breathe is the thought that you are on the other side of the world waiting for me."

She freezes, her eyes searching mine.

"You aren't the tether holding me down," I say, gripping her shoulders. "You are the anchor that keeps me from washing away. Without you, I'm just… I'm just a suit. I'm just ambition with no purpose. I'm a machine."

"You love your work," she whispers weaky.

"I like winning," I correct her. "But I love you. And winning means nothing if I have to lose you to do it."

"Edward…"

"I walked out," I tell her. "My father told me if I left, Lincoln would fire me. He told me I was throwing away the White House." Her eyes widen. "You… you left?" "I walked out in the middle of a briefing. I didn't pack. I didn't ask for permission. Because when I saw your message, when I thought for one second that I might lose you… none of it mattered. Not the election. Not the firm. None of it."

I take her face in my hands. Her skin is cold, wet with rain and tears. "Don't you dare tell me I'm better off without you. I am nothing without you. If you want to leave me because you don't love me anymore, say it. Look me in the eye and say it, and I will let you go."

I lean my forehead against hers. "But don't you dare leave me because you think you're doing me a favor."

VII. The Surrender

She stares at me. Her breath comes in jagged gasps. She is searching my face for a lie, for a hesitation, for the politician I might have become. But she finds only the boy she met on this cliff years ago.

The resolve in her eyes cracks. The nobility crumbles, leaving only the naked, terrifying need she has been hiding. "I thought…" she chokes out. "I thought it was the right thing to do."

"It's the wrong thing," I whisper. "It's the worst thing."

"I'm scared, Edward. I'm so scared of the distance."

"So am I. But we bridge it. We figure it out. I'll quit the firm if I have to. I'll move here. I'll consult remotely. I don't care. We make the rules."

She lets out a sound that is half-sob, half-laugh. "You'd really quit?"

"In a heartbeat."

She looks at me, and finally, the wall comes down. The strength she gathered to break her own heart dissolves. "I don't want you to quit," she whispers. "I just want you to come back to me."

"I'm here," I say. "I'm back."

She collapses into me. It isn't a gentle hug. It is a collision. She buries her face in my neck, gripping the lapels of my coat so hard her knuckles turn white. I wrap my arms around her, crushing her to me, trying to fuse our broken pieces back together.

We stand there in the rain, on the edge of the cliff, holding on for dear life. The wind howls around us, but for the first time in months, the storm inside me goes quiet.

"I love you," she sobs into my coat. "I love you so much it hurts." "I love you," I promise into her hair. "I'm not going anywhere."

VIII. The Aftermath

We stay there until the cold becomes dangerous. We walk back down the path, her hand gripped tightly in mine, as if she fears I might evaporate if she lets go.

We find a small tea house near the harbor that is still open. We sit in the corner, steaming mugs of barley tea between us. My coat is drying on the back of the chair. Her scarf is unspooled on the table. We look like shipwreck survivors.

"So," she says, tracing the rim of her cup. Her eyes are red, but clear. "You really walked out on Governor Lincoln?"

I smile. A real smile. "I did. My father looked like he was going to have a stroke." "He's going to be angry." "Furious." "Are you worried?"

I think about it. I think about the furious text messages currently populating my phone. I think about the headlines that might run tomorrow: Top Aide Abandons Campaign. I take a sip of the tea. It tastes of roasted grain and warmth. "No," I say. "I'm really not."

Jennie reaches across the table and takes my hand. "We have to figure this out," she says. "The logistics. The geography. I can't move to D.C., Edward. My life is here. My art is here."

"I know."

"And you can't leave D.C. completely. It's who you are."

"We'll compromise," I say. "I have leverage now. Lincoln needs me more than I need him. I'll demand telework. I'll demand two weeks here every month. And if he says no… then I find a new client."

"You make it sound so simple."

"It is simple," I look at her. "Everything is simple compared to the alternative of losing you."

She smiles—a small, tired, hopeful thing that lights up the dimly lit room. "Okay," she says softly. "Okay."

IX. The Promise

Later that night, we walk along the harbor wall. The rain has stopped, leaving the air scrubbed clean and sharp. The fishing boats bob in the dark water, their lights reflecting like submerged stars.

Jennie leans her head on my shoulder. We are walking in step, a rhythm we fell back into instantly.

"Will you stay?" she whispers. "For a few days?"

"I'll stay as long as it takes," I say. "I'll stay until you're sick of me."

She laughs, the sound vibrating against my side. "That might take a while."

I stop walking and turn her toward me one last time. The harbor lights illuminate her face—the face that saved me from becoming a ghost in a suit.

"I'm sorry I made you feel like you had to let me go," I say seriously. "I will spend the rest of my life making sure you never feel that way again."

She stands on her tiptoes and kisses me. It tastes of salt and tea and rain. It is a kiss of reclamation.

"Just don't disappear on me again, Edward," she whispers against my lips.

"Never," I vow.

I wrap my arm around her, and we turn back toward the lights of the town. My phone buzzes in my pocket. Lincoln. My father. The world. I don't reach for it. I leave it in the dark. I have everything I need right here.

Chapter Seventeen: The Border War

I. The Iceberg

Washington D.C. does not forgive. It remembers, it archives, and it waits.

I returned to the capital on a red-eye flight that landed in a gray, weeping dawn. The humidity of Seoul—that vibrant, living soup of garlic and diesel—was replaced by the sterile, air-conditioned chill of the Beltway. I didn't go to my apartment. I showered in the lounge at Dulles, drank three espressos that tasted like battery acid, and went straight to the campaign headquarters on K Street.

I was wearing the suit. It was the charcoal bespoke number my father had ordered for me before I left, the one meant to signal my ascension to the senior ranks. Before Korea, it would have felt like a costume, a stiff carapace designed to hold a shape I didn't possess. Now, as I fastened the cufflinks and knotted the silk tie, it felt different. It felt like armor. And I was going to need it.

When I walked into the war room at 7:30 a.m., the temperature seemed to drop ten degrees. The open-plan office was already buzzing. Phones were ringing, CNN was blaring from wall-mounted screens, and interns were sprinting with coffee trays. But as I passed the rows of desks, a ripple of silence followed me. Staffers looked down at their phones. Junior aides suddenly found fascinating things to study on the ceiling. The rumor mill, more efficient than any wire service, had been churning for days: The Golden Boy cracked. The Deputy Counsel went rogue. He flew to Korea for a girl in the middle of the primary season.

I ignored them. I walked straight to the glass-walled office at the end of the corridor. My father was waiting. He was standing by the window, looking out at the rain-slicked street. He didn't turn when I entered. The reflection in the glass showed a man who had aged ten years in ten days. His shoulders, usually squared with the confidence of a man who bills a thousand dollars an hour, were slumped.

"You're back," he said to the window. "I am." He turned slowly. His face was gray, the lines around his mouth etched deep with a mixture of disappointment and fear. "Did you get it out of your system?" I placed my leather briefcase on his desk. The sound was heavy, final. "It wasn't a virus, Dad. It was a life choice."

He scoffs, a sharp, dismissive sound that sounded like paper tearing. "It was a tantrum, Edward. A dangerous, adolescent tantrum. Governor Lincoln is not a man who tolerates instability in his inner circle. Do you have any idea the capital I had to spend to keep your desk from being cleared out?"

"I fixed the data breach before I left," I said calmly. "The campaign didn't lose a step. My team delivered the opposition research on Senator Kaine two days ahead of schedule."

"The campaign runs on perception!" he snapped, slamming his hand on the desk. "And the perception is that my son—the future of this firm, the Deputy Counsel to the next President—is chasing a painter across the Pacific like a lovesick teenager. You embarrassed us, Edward. You embarrassed me."

I looked at him. Really looked at him. For years, this man had been the monolith of my life. The arbiter of my worth. But looking at him now, terrified of a politician's displeasure, he looked small. "I'm sorry you feel embarrassed," I said. "But I'm not sorry I went."

He stared at me, stunned by the lack of contrition. He opened his mouth to speak, likely to invoke the family legacy, but his intercom buzzed. "Mr. Gray? The Governor is on the secure line. He wants Edward at the townhouse. Immediately."

My father paled. He looked at me with something close to panic. "He wants to see you personally," he whispered. "Edward, listen to me. If you want to salvage any scrap of your career, if you want to have a future in this city, you will go there, you will apologize, and you will listen more than you speak. Do you understand?"

I picked up my briefcase. "I understand perfectly," I said.

II. The Wedge

Governor John F. Lincoln's private townhouse in Georgetown is a masterclass in intimidation. It is not an office; it is a sanctuary of old power. Dark mahogany wainscoting, Persian rugs that muffle footsteps, the smell of pipe tobacco and legislative secrets.

I was ushered into the study by a silent aide who closed the heavy double doors behind me. Lincoln was sitting by the fireplace, though it was June and the AC was humming. He was reading a dossier, a glass of iced tea sweating on the coaster beside him. He didn't look up. I stood and waited. I used the silence to breathe. I thought of the cliffs at Haesindang. I thought of the ocean. I let the memory of the wind settle my pulse.

Finally, Lincoln closed the folder. He took off his reading glasses, folded them deliberately, and looked at me. His expression was not angry. It was worse. It was pitying.

"Edward," he said, his voice that famous, rich baritone that charmed voters in three states. "Sit." I sat in the leather wingback chair opposite him. "I hear Korea was... clarifying." "It was necessary, Governor." "For you, perhaps. For us? It was a distraction. We are six months out from the Iowa caucus. I need soldiers, Edward. Not poets."

He leaned forward, elbows on his knees, clasping his hands. He looked like a benevolent uncle about to explain why he had to put down the family dog. "I like you, Edward. You know that. Your father is a good grinder, but you... you have a mind like a diamond. Hard. Sharp. Brilliant. You see the board in a way others don't." "Thank you, sir." "But diamonds can shatter if you hit them at the wrong angle. This girl... Jennie... she's the wrong angle."

I kept my face impassive. "With all due respect, sir, my personal life is separate from my duties. My output hasn't suffered." "Your personal life is a national security concern when you are the Deputy Counsel to the future President," he interrupted, his voice turning steel-hard. The uncle was gone. The predator was back. "You are vetting Supreme Court nominees. You are handling classified donor data. I cannot have you compromised by a foreign national with no clearance and a penchant for distraction."

"She is an artist, Governor. Not a spy."

"Frankly, it doesn't matter what she is. She is a waste of your time. She is a fad. A boheJennien phase you're using to rebel against your father." He sat back, crossing his legs. "You need a partner who understands this world. Someone who can host a donor dinner. Someone like Sarah Mitchell. I saw you two at the gala. That is a power couple. That is a future."

I stiffen. The mention of Sarah—who was a friend, a colleague, and a road not taken—felt like a violation. "That is not your decision to make."

Lincoln smiled. It was a terrifying smile because it lacked all warmth. It was the smile of a man who believed he was the architect of reality. "Oh, but it is, Edward. Because I make the world work. And I've decided to help you focus."

He reached into a drawer in the side table and slid a piece of paper across the polished wood. It was a photocopy of a visa application. Applicant: Jennie Kim. Visa Type: O-1B (Individuals with Extraordinary Ability in the Arts). Sponsor: The Meridian Gallery, New York.

My heart leaped into my throat. She had applied. She was trying to come here. She hadn't told me—probably wanting to surprise me. "She applied last week," Lincoln said, watching my face closely. "Talented girl. The gallery in Chelsea wants to sponsor her. It's a strong application. Her portfolio is impressive."

I reached for the paper, but Lincoln placed his hand over it. "But," he continued, his voice lowering to a conspiratorial whisper, "the State Department has concerns. There are... irregularities."

"What irregularities?" I asked, my voice cold.

"Potential ties to radical student groups in Seoul," Lincoln lied smoothly. "Concerns about her financial stability. A fear that she intends to overstay her visa and seek permanent residence through marriage. It's going to be denied, Edward."

I stared at him. The room went quiet, save for the ticking of the grandfather clock. "You're blocking her," I whispered.

"I'm protecting my investment," Lincoln said calmly. "I made a call. A favor for a friend. The Consular Officer in Seoul has been instructed to flag her application. Section 214(b)—failure to demonstrate non-immigrant intent. It's a catch-all. Very hard to appeal."

Rage, white-hot and blinding, flared in my chest. He wasn't just interfering; he was weaponizing the federal government to break a girl's heart. "And any subsequent applications," Lincoln added, twisting the knife, "tourist, business, fiancé… they will be flagged for indefinite administrative processing. She will never step foot on American soil, Edward. Not while I have influence."

He leaned back, satisfied. "You can't visit her if you're working eighty hours a week for me. And she can't visit you if she can't cross the border. The distance will do its work. Six months, and you'll forget the color of her eyes. You'll thank me."

He gestured to the door. "This is for your own good. You're too brilliant to be tethered to a painter in Mapo-gu. Now, go home. Get some sleep. We have a briefing on the Iowa numbers at 0800."

III. The Doctrine

I looked at the paper under his hand. I looked at Jennie's face in the passport photo. She looked serious. Unarmed. I thought of the park. I thought of her laughing at the phallic statues, teaching me that reverence and laughter could coexist. I thought of the way she held my hand in the bookstore. And then I looked at Governor Lincoln. A man who thought people were chess pieces.

He had made a fatal error. He assumed I was still my father's son. He assumed I was a lawyer who followed the rules. He forgot that he had hired me because I was the man who found the patterns no one else saw. He forgot that I was the one who knew where the bodies were buried because I was the one who dug the graves.

I didn't stand up. I reached into my briefcase. My hand did not shake. "You're right, Governor," I said softly.

He nodded, expecting capitulation. He picked up his iced tea. "I usually am. It's a burden, but someone has to bear it."

"I am brilliant," I said. "I am the guy who finds the patterns. I am the guy who reads the footnotes. I am the guy who cross-references the metadata."

Lincoln frowned slightly, the glass pausing halfway to his mouth. "Yes. That's why you're here."

"So, three months ago, when you asked me to vet your family history for the campaign—to 'scrub the lines,' as you put it, to ensure there were no surprises before the primaries—I did. I scrubbed everything. Your finances. Your brother's DUIs. Your wife's family trust."

I pulled out a blue folder. It was thin. Unassuming. I placed it on top of Jennie's visa application.

"What is this?" Lincoln asked. His voice had lost its paternal warmth.

"Immigration and Nationality Act, Section 212(a)(3)(E)," I cited from memory, my voice echoing in the quiet room. "Participants in Nazi persecution, genocide, or the commission of any act of torture or extrajudicial killing. It renders an alien permanently inadmissible and deportable. And it renders anyone who aids them in concealing that fact subject to criminal prosecution for visa fraud."

Lincoln's face went pale. He set the glass down. It rattled against the coaster. "What are you talking about?"

"Your wife," I said calmly. "Elena. A wonderful woman. Her grandfather, Heinrich Vogel. He entered the United States in 1948 via Operation Paperclip's side channels. He listed his occupation as a 'low-level chemist' for a paint manufacturer."

"He was a chemist," Lincoln snapped. "He worked for a pharmaceutical company in Ohio for thirty years. He was a deacon in his church."

"He was a chemist," I agreed. "At IG Farben. Specifically, the Buna-Werke division at Monowitz. The records were supposed to be destroyed, Governor, but the East German archives were digitized last year. I found his payroll number. I found his signature on the requisition forms for the synthetic rubber testing."

I opened the folder. There was a photocopy of a faded German document. A signature: H. Vogel. And next to it, a requisition order for labor from the adjacent concentration camp.

"He didn't just work there," I said, my voice dropping to a whisper. "He managed the shift rotation for the forced laborers. He signed off on the 'exhaustion' reports."

The silence in the room was deafening. It was the sound of a political career flatlining.

"Elena doesn't know," Lincoln whispered. It wasn't a denial. It was a realization.

"I know she doesn't," I said. "But you do. Because you signed her naturalization paperwork when you sponsored her citizenship update ten years ago. You swore under penalty of perjury that there were no undisclosed issues with her family's entry status. You buried it."

Lincoln stared at the document. His hands were gripping the arms of his chair so hard his knuckles were white. "You wouldn't."

"If you weaponize the immigration system against Jennie," I said, leaning forward, "I will weaponize it against you. I will leak this to the Times. I will leak it to the Post. I will hand-deliver it to the Department of Justice."

"It would destroy Elena," he hissed. "It would destroy the campaign."

"Yes," I said. "It would. It would paint you as a man covering up for a Nazi war criminal to protect his own ambition. You wouldn't just lose Iowa, John. You would lose everything."

I sat back. "You said diamonds shatter if you hit them at the wrong angle. You hit me at the wrong angle."

IV. The Capitulation

For a long minute, neither of us moved. Lincoln looked at me. He looked for the bluff. He looked for the hesitation of the young associate who wanted to please his father. He found none of it. He found a man who had stood in front of a giant wooden phallus and learned that shame was a choice.

Lincoln exhaled. It was a long, shuddering sound. He closed the blue folder. He picked up Jennie's visa application. He picked up his phone. He dialed a number.

"It's Lincoln," he said into the receiver. "The Kim application. O-1B. Yes." He paused, watching me. "I've reviewed the file personally. The irregularities were a clerical error on our end. She is a priority applicant. Expedite it. I want it stamped by close of business in Seoul."

He listened for a moment. "Yes. A ten-year multi-entry visa. And flag her for Global Entry approval. We want talent like that in the country."

He hung up. He slid the application back to me. "Done," he said.

I picked up the blue folder. I didn't hand it to him. I put it back in my briefcase. "Thank you, Governor."

Lincoln looked at me, and for the first time, there was genuine respect in his eyes. It was the respect of a wolf recognizing another wolf. "You kept that file," he said. "You had it the whole time. Why didn't you use it to get a promotion? To get a raise?"

"Because I didn't care about those things," I said, standing up. "I only care about this."

"You're a dangerous man, Edward," Lincoln said softly. "I underestimated you." "Don't do it again."

I turned to leave. "Edward," he called out. I stopped at the door. "Your father," Lincoln said. "He thinks you're soft. He thinks you're broken." "I know." "Send him in," Lincoln said. "I need to explain the new chain of command to him."

V. The Shift

My father was waiting in the hallway, pacing. He looked like a man waiting for a firing squad. When I emerged, he rushed over, scanning my face for signs of ruin. "Well?" he demanded. "Did you apologize? Is he firing us?"

"He wants to see you, Dad," I said calm. "Oh god," my father muttered. "He's going to terminate the retainer."

He brushed past me, smoothing his hair, putting on his subservient face. I waited. I waited ten minutes. When the door opened, my father walked out. He looked dazed. He looked at me as if he had never seen me before.

"What did he say?" I asked.

My father swallowed hard. "He said… he said that you are indispensable." He shook his head, confused. "He said that I am to leave you alone. He said that if you want to fly to the moon to visit a girl, I am to charter the rocket."

My father stepped closer. "He said… he said I should be learning from you." I looked at my father. The giant. The monolith. "I'm going home, Dad," I said. "I have a video call in an hour." "With the girl?" "With Jennie."

My father hesitated. Then, for the first time in his life, he stepped aside to let me pass. "Okay," he whispered. "Okay."

VI. The Reunion

Two weeks later. Dulles International Airport. Arrivals Terminal.

I am not wearing a suit. I am wearing jeans and a sweater. I am holding a sign, though she doesn't need it. The doors slide open. Passengers stream out—tired businessmen, families with strollers. And then, her.

Jennie. She is wearing a long coat and carrying a portfolio case. She looks tired. She looks small against the vastness of the American terminal. She scans the crowd. She sees me. She drops the case.

She runs. I catch her. I lift her off the ground. She buries her face in my neck, smelling of plane air and citrus. "I got it," she sobs into my shoulder. "I got the visa. They expedited it. I don't understand how, but they did."

I hold her tighter. I look over her shoulder at the exit signs. "I told you," I whisper into her hair. "I told you I wouldn't disappear."

She pulls back, looking at my face. She touches my cheek. "You look different," she says. "How?" "You look…" She searches for the word. "Formidable."

I smile. I take her bag. I take her hand. "Come on," I say. "Let's go home. I have a lot to tell you."

We walk toward the exit. I think of the blue folder locked in my safe. I think of Lincoln's face. I think of the suit hanging in my closet. It is still a suit. But it is no longer a cage. It is just clothes. And I am the one wearing it.

VII. A Father's Wish

The weeks following my return to D.C. were a blur of quiet reclamation. For three weeks, Jennie lived in my apartment, her presence slowly filling the sterile corners of my life with color. My mother adored her immediately—perhaps because she saw in Jennie the same spark she had surrendered years ago.

Michael flew down from Boston for dinner one evening. He stood in my living room, looking at a charcoal sketch Jennie had done of the Potomac. He didn't say "I told you so." He just smiled, a genuine, vindicated expression. "You held on, Ed," he said, clinking his glass against mine. "I'm glad you held on."

I did not call Lorenzo or Damion. The cruelty of the airport, though a decade old, still felt sharp. I realized then that some friendships are for a season, and some are for a lifetime. I had outgrown the season of cynicism.

But the bubble burst on a Tuesday. It was a bright, indifferent spring day when my father collapsed in his office at the firm.

It was autonomic failure—a sudden, dangerous drop in blood pressure caused by the advanced progression of his Parkinson's. The disease he had hidden for so long was no longer whispering; it was shouting.

I went to the hospital immediately. By the time I arrived, the doctors had stabilized him. They were adjusting his dopamine agonists, bringing his pressure back up. He wasn't dying—not today—but the event was a terrifying bellwether.

Dr. Evans pulled me into the hallway, his expression grave. "He's recovering, Edward. We can discharge him in a few days. But you need to understand the trajectory. The autonomic issues are starting. Realistically? You have four, maybe six good years before the decline becomes unmanageable."

Four years. It sounded like an eternity and a second all at once.

I walked into his room. He was awake, sitting up slightly, looking pale but alert. The titan was still there, but the armor was gone. In the bed lay a man who finally understood that his time was finite.

He watched me enter. His voice was a rasp, but steady.

"Edward."

I took his hand. It was warm again, the crisis having passed. "I'm here, Dad. You're going to be okay. They're releasing you this week."

He nodded, dismissing the medical details with a wave of his hand. He pulled me closer, his grip weak but insistent. He looked at me, really looked at me, stripped of the expectations and the disappointed sighs.

"I know what the doctors are saying," he whispered. "I know the clock is ticking louder than it used to."

He closed his eyes for a moment, then opened them, fixing me with a gaze of startling intensity.

"Edward, as my only son, I have always wanted the best for you. I thought the best was the firm. I thought it was power. But lying here… the view changes." He squeezed my hand. "I want to see the next generation of Grays arrive while I can still hold them. Son, when are you going to marry Jennie and ensure this family continues?"

I stared at him, stunned. The air left my lungs. For a decade, I had fought him for the right to choose her. And now, facing the twilight of his life, he wasn't just accepting her; he was asking for her.

I squeezed his hand back, and for the first time in ten years, my heart didn't just feel full. It felt free.

"Soon, Dad," I smiled, tears blurring my vision. "Very soon. You'll be there to see it."

Chapter Eighteen: The Marriage by the Sea

I. The Sacred and the Profane

The wind at Haesindang Park does not care about dignity. It whips off the Sea of Japan—the East Sea—carrying the bite of salt and the ancient, fishy tang of drying squid. It is a wind that gets under your collar and messes up your hair, a wind that feels like a rough, playful hand.

It was fitting, I thought, as I adjusted my tie in the reflection of a polished granite marker. We were getting married in a place that defied every convention my old life held sacred. Haesindang. The "Penis Park." A cliffside shrine dedicated to a virgin ghost who could only be appeased by the carving of wooden phalluses. It was a place of tragedy, yes, but also of bawdy, undeniable life. It was absurd. It was beautiful. And it was exactly where we needed to be.

I looked up the path. The ceremony was set on a small plateau overlooking the crashing waves, surrounded by the park's famous statues—totems of fertility carved with grinning, exaggerated gusto.

My father stood near the edge of the clearing. He was wearing a linen suit, lighter than his usual armor, but he still looked like a man trying to solve a complex litigation problem. He was staring at a six-foot-tall wooden carving of a phallus that had been whimsically fashioned into a park bench. He looked at it. He looked at the ocean. He looked at it again.

"It's cultural, Dad," I said, coming up beside him.

He jumped slightly. "It's… certainly distinct," he said. He cleared his throat. "The view is magnificent, Edward. The water. It's very clear."

"It is."

He turned to me. The year had softened him. Or perhaps, realizing he couldn't control me had forced him to simply know me. The fear was gone from his eyes, replaced by a cautious curiosity. "Your mother is over there," he gestured vaguely toward the treeline.

"She's explaining the symbolism to the Kims. I believe she's had two glasses of champagne already."

"Good for her."

He hesitated, then reached out and straightened my lapel. It was a reflex, but his hand lingered. "Lincoln sent a car," he said quietly. "Security detail is sweeping the lower lot. He's actually coming."

"I know."

My father shook his head, a small, baffled smile touching his lips. "You forced the future President of the United States to attend a wedding at a fertility shrine in Samcheok. I still don't know if that makes you a genius or a madman."

"A bit of both," I said. "Mostly, I just wanted him to see what he almost destroyed."

II. The Assembly

The guests began to settle. It was a small gathering, a patchwork of two worlds stitched together by the sound of the surf.

Jennie's mother was there, a formidable woman in a pale blue hanbok that fluttered in the breeze. She was holding a handkerchief to her nose, her eyes red-rimmed and shining. For months she had been skeptical of the "American lawyer," but today, watching her daughter instruct the cellist, she looked like she had won a war.

Sohee was there, too. She stood near the back, wearing a sharp black jumpsuit, holding a cigarette she hadn't lit. When our eyes met, she didn't look away. She offered a small, crooked smile—a peace offering. We had talked, briefly, when I first returned. There were no apologies, just an acknowledgment that we were two people who had used each other to survive a lonely winter, and that summer had finally come.

And then, the friends. Michael stood at my side as best man, looking vindicated; he was the only one who had never told me to move on. Lorenzo and Damion were there, too, seated in the second row. They were quieter than usual, stripped of their old cynicism, watching the "impossible" happen with a look of genuine respect.

Mr. Park, the owner of the guesthouse where I had first stayed, was wearing a tuxedo that was at least twenty years out of date, beaming like he was giving away his own son. And Min-su, the fisherman who had sold me that first, terrible bottle of soju, stood with his wife, looking uncomfortable in a tie but very happy to be near the open bar.

A black SUV rolled quietly to the edge of the restricted service road. The doors opened, and Governor John F. Lincoln stepped out. He was flanked by two men in sunglasses who looked scanningly at the wooden statues with deep professional suspicion.

Lincoln walked over. He looked older than he had in his study, the weight of the upcoming general election sitting on his shoulders. But as he took in the scene—the eccentric carvings, the endless blue horizon—his face relaxed.

"Edward," he said, extending a hand. "Governor. You made it." "I had a trade summit in Seoul. I couldn't miss the... unique venue." He glanced at the phallic bench my father had been studying. A dry chuckle escaped him. "You certainly know how to control the narrative, don't you? If the press gets a photo of me next to that, I lose the evangelical vote in a landslide."

"Then we better make sure they don't," I said. "I brought you something," Lincoln said, motioning to his aide, who handed me a small, heavy box. "Vintage. 1948. A good year for new beginnings." "Thank you, John." He nodded, his eyes drifting to the altar. "She's worth the trouble, Edward. I see that now. Don't mess it up."

III. The Sculpture

The music shifted. The cellist began a low, mournful melody that slowly climbed into something bright and soaring.

I took my place. We did not have a priest. We did not have a minister. We had decided to speak only to each other, with the ocean as our witness.

And we did not have a cross.

Standing at the center of the clearing, framed by the sky, was the sculpture Jennie had made. It was small, perhaps three feet high, set on a simple stone plinth. It was carved from a single piece of driftwood she had found on this very beach the day I returned.

It was abstract, twisting and turning in on itself. At the base, the wood was rough, scarred by the salt and the rocks—jagged, dark, wounded. But as the form rose, the wood became smooth. It had been sanded and polished until it glowed with the warmth of amber. The two twisting forms didn't merge into one; they remained distinct, spiraling around each other, supporting each other, rising together toward a tapered point that seemed to catch the light of the sun.

It wasn't perfect. It was raw. It looked like something that had survived a storm.

Jennie walked down the aisle.

She wasn't wearing a traditional white gown. She wore a dress of cream-colored silk, hand-painted at the hem with strokes of indigo ink that looked like crashing waves. She wore no veil. Her face was open to the wind, her dark hair loose.

When she reached me, she didn't take my hand immediately. She looked at me. She looked at the suit I was wearing—not the charcoal armor of Washington, but a softer blue linen that moved with the air. She smiled, and the breath I hadn't realized I was holding rushed out of me.

IV. The Vow

We stood before the sculpture. The wind quieted, as if the ocean itself was leaning in to listen.

Jennie reached out and touched the rough base of the wood. Her fingers traced the scars in the grain.

"You asked me once," she said, her voice clear and carrying over the sound of the surf, "why I paint things that are broken. Why I like the ink when it spills."

She looked at my parents, then at Lincoln, and finally settled her gaze on me. Her eyes were dark and fierce.

"I told you that perfection is a lie. That the only things that matter are the things that survive." She took my hand then. Her palm was

150

warm, her grip strong. The hand of an artist, stained faintly with charcoal even today.

"Edward, we are not perfect. We are two people who were running away from different things. You were running from your father's shadow. I was running from the fear of being ordinary."

She paused, blinking back tears.

"But we found each other in the running. We collided. And we broke. And that was the best thing that could have happened."

She turned to the sculpture, running her hand up from the rough base to the smooth, polished spiral at the top.

"This is us," she said. "Rough at the bottom. Smooth at the top. But the same wood."

She turned back to me.

"I vow to never ask you to be unbroken," she said. "I vow to love your cracks. I vow to fight with you, to challenge you, and to never let you hide behind a suit again."

She took a breath, and then she delivered the words that she had carved into the base of the wood, words that would define the rest of our lives.

"Because to love," she said softly, "is to carve something out of what was once a wound."

I felt the tears hot on my face. I didn't wipe them away. I looked at my father, and saw he was weeping openly, his hand clutching my mother's. I looked at Lincoln, who was staring at the ground, looking unusually mortal.

"Jennie," I said, my voice thick. "I lived my whole life thinking that life was a performance. That if I didn't say the right lines, I would be written out of the script. You taught me that there is no script. There is only the paint, and the canvas, and the courage to make a mess."

I squeezed her hand.

"I vow to be your canvas. I vow to be your anchor when the current is strong. And I vow to never, ever let them close the border between us again."

V. The Horizon

The applause was swallowed by the wind, but the joy remained.

Later, as the sun began to dip into the mountains behind us, casting long, purple shadows across the water, the party moved to the lower pavilion. There was wine. There was laughter. My father was awkwardly discussing tax law with Min-su, who didn't understand a word of English but kept pouring my father shots of soju. Lincoln had departed, leaving behind the ghost of his power and a very expensive bottle of wine.

I stood by the railing, looking out at the darkening sea. The lighthouse in the distance began to blink.

Jennie came up beside me. She wrapped her arms around my waist and rested her head on my shoulder.

She whispered "Are you happy, Edward?"

I looked at the horizon. I thought of the office on K Street. I thought of the silence in my apartment in D.C. I thought of the terrifying, exhilarating uncertainty of the future. I wasn't the Deputy Counsel anymore. I was just a man, standing by the sea, holding the woman I loved.

"I'm not happy," I said, turning to kiss the top of her head. "I'm real. And that's better."

She laughed, the sound bright and free, rising up into the twilight to mix with the cry of the gulls.

"Come on," she said, pulling me toward the music. "Your dad is trying to dance. We can't miss this."

We ran back toward the light, leaving the ocean to churn in the dark, carving the rocks, endlessly, into something new.

Chapter Nineteen: The Pilgrimage

I. The Quiet Victory

The suburbs of Boston are quiet in a way that Washington never is. In D.C., silence is terrified anticipation; it means a scandal is breaking or a bill is dying. In Wellesley, silence just means the snow is falling, or the neighbors are sleeping.

I stood on the back porch of our colonial revival, a mug of coffee warming my hands against the October chill. Inside, the house was waking up. I could hear the thud of small feet, the clatter of a cereal bowl, the low hum of the radio.

It had been ten years.

In that time, the world had turned over several times. I had kept my promise to myself, and to Jennie. I didn't go back to the daily grinder of K Street. Instead, I ran John Lincoln's presidential campaign from a converted brownstone in Beacon Hill. I was the "Strategist in Absentia," the man who refused to move to the capital, the man who dialed into the Situation Room via encrypted video link because he had a soccer game to coach at 4:00 p.m.

We won. We won big. Lincoln took forty-two states. On election night, amidst the confetti and the screaming crowds at the hotel, the President-elect had hugged me and whispered, "You were right. The view is better from the outside."

I looked at the leaves turning gold in the yard. My hair matched the frost on the grass now—streaks of iron-gray at the temples. My soul felt grayer, too, but not in the way of decay. It was the gray of worn stone, of something that has weathered storms and come out solid. I wasn't the sharp, brittle diamond Lincoln had once described. I was granite.

II. The Ambassador of Ink

The back door slid open. Jennie stepped out, wrapping a wool cardigan around her silk pajamas. She looked different, too. The frantic, hungry energy of her twenties had settled into a potent, regal confidence.

"You're thinking about the trip," she said, leaning against the railing. "I'm thinking about the logistics. A twelve-hour flight with Leo and Sophie is a strategic nightmare I wasn't trained for."

She laughed, sipping from my mug. "They'll be fine. Leo wants to see the squid boats. Sophie just wants to eat convenience store ramen."

Jennie had built a kingdom here. Her studio, The Slate & Silk Collective, occupied a massive loft in the South End. It wasn't just an art school; it was a cultural phenomenon. She taught traditional ink wash techniques to uptight New Englanders, teaching them how to lose control of the brush.

But the irony—the beautiful, delicious irony—was her official title.

Three years ago, the South Korean Ministry of Culture, the same bureaucratic entity that had once flagged her visa as a risk, had approached her. They wanted to rebrand their regional tourism. They wanted someone who understood the intersection of traditional folklore and modern art.

They named Jennie Kim the Cultural Ambassador for the Gangwon Province. Her specific portfolio included the preservation and promotion of folk shrines. specifically, Haesindang Park. She gave lectures at Harvard on the "duality of the sacred and the profane," legitimizing the very place that had once been our secret refuge.

"The Ministry sent the itinerary," she said. "They want a photo op at the entrance. Just us. No press." "And the kids?" "The kids," she smiled mischievously, "are going to get a very memorable biology lesson."

III. The Return

The drive from Incheon to Samcheok had improved in a decade. New tunnels cut through the mountains, turning a winding ordeal into a smooth glide through the spine of the peninsula.

Leo was nine, possessed of a solemn curiosity that reminded me painfully of my own father. Sophie was six, a chaotic ball of joy who resembled no one but herself.

When we pulled into the parking lot of Haesindang Park, the sea air hit us instantly—that same biting, salty, fish-heavy wind that I had breathed on the worst day of my life, and on the best.

"Is this the place?" Leo asked, looking at the steep path winding up the cliff. "This is the place," I said.

We began the climb. The park had changed slightly—new railings, a fresh coat of paint on the visitor center—but the soul of it was untouched. It was still a shrine to longing.

As we crested the hill and entered the main garden, the statues came into view. Dozens of them. Giant, carved wooden phalluses. Some laughing, some stoic, some shaped like benches, some shaped like cannons.

I tensed, the old reflex of American puritanism twitching in my spine. I looked at the kids.

Sophie stopped dead in her tracks. She pointed to a ten-foot-tall totem with a face carved into the tip. "It's a mushroom!" she squealed. "A giant daddy mushroom!"

Leo frowned, adjusting his glasses. "It looks like a rocket," he corrected. "But it's made of wood. That's not aerodynamic."

Jennie caught my eye. She was biting her lip to keep from laughing aloud. "They are totems, Leo," she said smoothly, walking over to them. "They represent life. Energy. The wish for things to grow."

"Can I climb it?" Sophie asked. "Absolutely not," I said quickly. "Maybe the small one," Jennie countered.

IV. The Reconciliation

We walked further, past the crowds of tourists who were giggling and taking selfies. We moved toward the cliff edge, away from the spectacle, to the quiet spot where we had said our vows.

The wooden sculpture Jennie had made for our wedding was gone, taken back to Boston to sit on our mantle. But the plinth remained, weathered by ten years of salt spray.

I stood there, looking out at the East Sea. The waves hammered the rocks below, the white foam boiling in the dark blue water.

Ten years ago, I had stood here terrified that I was throwing my life away. I thought faith was following the rules—my father's rules, Lincoln's rules, the rules of a polite society. I thought freedom was a dangerous, chaotic thing that destroyed careers.

I watched my children running in the grass near the edge of the safety rail. Sophie was chasing a dragonfly. Leo was examining the grain of the wood on a bench, likely analyzing its structural integrity.

I felt a profound settling in my chest. A quietus.

Faith and freedom were not enemies. They were partners. Faith was the trust that the boat would float; freedom was the courage to untie the rope. I had needed both. I had needed the discipline to build a life, and the wildness to choose the right one.

Jennie had moved away from the kids. She had her camera out—a heavy, professional Leica. She was photographing the horizon, capturing the exact moment the light hit the water. She was focused, her brow furrowed, in that trance state she always entered before she created something.

She looked up, sensing my gaze. She lowered the camera. The wind whipped her hair across her face. She looked older, yes. There were lines around her eyes that hadn't been there when we were twenty-five. But she was more beautiful for them. She was a masterpiece that had been lived in.

I walked over to her. "What are you thinking?" she asked.

I looked back at the giant, ridiculous, wooden statues standing guard over the ocean. I looked at our children, laughing as they played tag around a fertility totem.

"I'm thinking that my father was wrong," I said. "He told me this place was a detour. He didn't know it was the destination."

Jennie smiled. She reached out and took my hand. Her palm was still warm, still strong. "It's a good pilgrimage, Edward."

I squeezed her hand. The sun was beginning to set, casting long shadows across the park, turning the wooden carvings into silhouettes against the burning orange sky. It was absurd. It was holy. It was ours.

I pulled her closer, watching the kids run back toward us, their laughter carrying over the sound of the waves.

Every spring, they return to the place that made them blush—and believe.

It started as a post-graduation trip. It became a promise that would take ten years to keep.

Fresh out of undergrad, Edward Gray went to South Korea with his friends, looking for adventure and a deeper understanding of the world. What he found was Haesindang Park—a seaside shrine to fertility and longing—and Jennie Kim, an artist who saw the world in strokes of wild, unapologetic ink. For one glorious summer, Edward forgot the weight of his last name. He forgot the plan.

But the plan was waiting.

Bound by duty to a demanding father and a family legacy he couldn't escape, Edward returned to the U.S. He buried the memory of the ocean and the girl, molding himself into the man he was supposed to be. Years later, he has succeeded. He is the "Golden Boy" of Washington D.C., a brilliant legal mind and Deputy Counsel to the future President. He wears the bespoke suits. He wins the hard cases. He is a masterpiece of control.

But the heart has a long memory.

When Edward risks everything to fly back to Korea and reclaim the life he left behind, the political machine strikes back. Governor John F. Lincoln, fearing a distraction during a critical election year, weaponizes the federal government to keep the lovers apart, turning the border into a prison wall.

They think Edward is just another ambitious lawyer who will follow orders. They forgot that beneath the suit lies the heart of the boy who once stood on a cliff in Samcheok and learned that love is stronger than law.

From the neon nostalgia of Seoul to the cutthroat corridors of K Street, **The Unruly Promise** is a story about the geography of desire—and the secrets one man will use to tear down the borders between him and the woman he loves.

About the Author

E. E. Frazer is a storyteller who views fiction as a journey-one that transports readers across borders and leaves a lasting impact on the heart. His approach to writing is deeply rooted in a philosophy passed down by his mother, which has shaped his worldview: "Mental travel requires no passport or money, simply curiosity about people and culture. Watch the news and listen to the radio with that curiosity in mind, and you can travel the entire world."

That curiosity has defined E.E Frazer's life and career. A seasoned executive, he draws upon a rich professional background as a former CEO and Senior Vice President across multiple industries. His intellectual foundation includes degrees in Political Science, Law, and a Master's degree. He is a world traveler, who has lived in 5 countries, spanning two continents.

Today, he blends that global perspective with a poet's sensibility, crafting stories that invite readers to travel the world through his words and explore the unmapped territories of human connection.

www.ingramcontent.com/pod-product-compliance
Lightning Source LLC
Chambersburg PA
CBHW060648260626
47161CB00008B/3045